DEDICATION AND THANKS

*I dedicate this book to my parents and my four siblings,
who are no longer with us. They taught me that the real
reason for celebrating Christmas was to celebrate the birth
of Jesus. Santa Claus also played a role. It wasn't easy for
this author to stop believing in the jolly ol' guy.*

Introduction

The word *Christmas* grabs my attention and makes me smile. It's my favorite time of year because it was always a time of joy when I was growing up.

As kids, my siblings and I had to recite or sing something at the Christmas Eve service at our church every year. Mother made sure we always had sparkly new dresses to wear for the occasion. After the service, we were given a paper bag containing a large orange and chocolate candy.

When we arrived home, we lined up to go into the living room, where we knew Santa had left us gifts while we were in church. The gifts were unwrapped but arranged lovingly beneath the tree. I was the youngest, so I was always the first in line to collect a gift.

This tradition continued until I married and had two sons, Joel and Jason. My husband and I blended our family traditions so that our kids, too, would grow up with warm memories of Christmas.

I've learned through the years that my reading fans love Christmas as much as I do. I feel their joy. I love to hear how others spend their Christmas and what traditions they celebrate from all over the world.

I enjoyed writing these short stories and poems. I hope you like them also and will let me know which one was your favorite. Maybe someday you will write your own Christmas story and pass it along for others to read.

My family and I wish you a very merry Christmas.

~Ann

NATURE'S CHRISTMAS

Goodbye, pretty leaves of orange and gold.

Put on your coat as the winter blows cold.

You will be warm with a blanket of snow.

The warmth will comfort you more than you know.

Along comes the season of red holly berries.

They last a lot longer than red summer cherries.

The greens of the fir, cedar, and pine

Fondly remind you that it's Christmastime.

I have to say it's the best time of year

With the sounds of music, children, and cheer.

Until we wait for spring to arrive

I can live off Christmas and perfectly thrive.

The Cemetery Quilter

I woke up when I heard Mrs. Newberry leave her downstairs apartment at nine o'clock, like she did every morning. She was too old to work. Where did she go?

I'd been renting the second-floor flat from Mrs. Newberry for nearly a year. She was friendly enough when I'd run into her, but it became clear early on that she was a private person and I should mind my own business. We mostly maintained a businesslike relationship until I'd bring her something special to eat. I baked her some coffee chocolate chip cookies a few times. She liked them enough to hint around for the recipe. My friend Andi shared the recipe for these cookies many years ago, and it was interesting watching folks taste that first bite because the coffee added a unique twist. Usually Mrs. Newberry would accept the cookies at the door and then shut the door immediately. Never once did she invite me inside. Part of me wanted to get to know her, but the other part told me to mind my own business.

As a woman living alone, I certainly respected Mrs. Newberry's wishes. I wasn't exactly a social butterfly either.

After my fifteen-year marriage to Paul ended in divorce, I sold most everything I had to simplify my life. The divorce was peaceful once we realized we wanted different things in life. He assured me he'd be there for me, even after moving to Utah. We rarely communicated, but I'd heard rumors he may have gotten remarried.

As a freelance writer, I wanted a quiet neighborhood near a park where I could find solace in writing. Mrs. Newberry's upstairs flat seemed like the perfect place. A friend told me about this well-maintained neighborhood occupied mostly by senior residents. I'd never had anything against children, but I was happy to live in this neighborhood of older adults.

On Thanksgiving, the wind was blowing the leaves in every direction. The colorful foliage inspired me this time of year, but I dreaded the upcoming winter. Christmas passed too quickly.

Our quiet street had little traffic and felt safe for walking. One direction led to a lovely park, and the other led to a cemetery. I didn't walk at any particular time of day. My ambles were based more on when I wanted to stretch my legs a bit.

Mrs. Newberry returned from her daily walks around noon. She'd carry the same red-and-white polka-dot tote bag that was large enough to hold just a few groceries. The bag seemed an odd choice for an 80-some-year-old woman.

Some neighbors were starting to put out their Christmas lights. Mrs. Newberry had told me once that she had candles she'd give me to place in each window for the holiday. They'd add the perfect touch for this old house. I hung a simple wreath on my door. Inside my apartment, lights were aglow on my tree and mantel.

When I returned from having Thanksgiving dinner with Aunt Amanda, Mrs. Newberry was getting back at the same time. I smiled and asked if she was having a nice Thanksgiving, and she said she was. She reminded me that she'd have my candles by my doorstep tomorrow. I thanked her and told her I'd place them in the windows that evening. Just like that, our communication ended, and she let herself inside the apartment.

My apartment had a screened-in porch, which I enjoyed immensely. It held a couch, a chair, and a desk I used to write on nice days. With the cooler weather coming, I was going to have to close up my porch for the winter.

As I put Aunt Amanda's leftovers away, I heard a siren. Stepping outside, I spotted a couple police cars and some fellow nosy neighbors. I always secretly hoped I'd witness a crime I could weave into a story. There was nothing to witness tonight, though. With no action in sight, I returned indoors and watched some TV before it was time for bed.

The next morning, I rose earlier than usual so I could begin my Christmas shopping. I was dressed when I heard Mrs. Newberry exit her apartment. My watch told me it was nine o'clock. She was right on schedule. I felt the urge to follow her and see for myself who she was meeting or where she might be going. I quickly threw on my coat, grabbed my purse, and started out a good distance behind her. It was thirty-eight degrees, so I didn't imagine she'd be walking too far.

She entered the ornate gate with the sign marking Heavenly Cemetery. I followed but chose to hide behind various tall stones so she wouldn't spot me. After a short while, she stopped and began talking. I looked around but didn't see anyone. She reached inside her bag and withdrew a cushion, which she placed on a stone bench near one of the tombstones. She was here to visit with a loved one.

Mrs. Newberry continued talking, but I couldn't hear what she was saying. I watched her pull out a quilt and needles and place it on her lap. I stood there shivering in disbelief as she began quilting in the middle of the cemetery. I knew she was a quilter because I'd occasionally see a quilt hanging on her outside clothesline, but I'd never known anyone who quilted among the deceased.

A couple came over to talk to Mrs. Newberry for a few minutes. They laughed at something she said and then left. She poured herself a cup of what I assumed was coffee from the thermos she had tucked in her bag. She offered some to a man who was nearby. The two of them seemed to know one another and engaged in conversation for a while. I needed to get going before she noticed me. I didn't want to interrupt her visit, and I was getting chilly. I hadn't thought to bring something hot to sip.

I'd never entered this cemetery before today. It was actually quite lovely. Most of the gravestones were old, and many were already adorned with poinsettias and wreaths for the holidays. I turned around and headed home, wondering about Mrs. Newberry's ritual.

The trip to the cemetery this morning wasn't something I'd planned. Shopping was, and I thought I'd better get to it. I grabbed my keys and headed out, all the while thinking about Mrs. Newberry and who she was visiting. Snowflakes began falling for the first time this season. Would Mrs. Newberry cut her visit short today because of the weather?

I waited another week before I purposefully arranged to meet her as she returned from her walk.

"Oh, hello, Mrs. Newberry. I have some coffee chocolate chip cookies for you."

"How sweet of you. I do enjoy them."

I smiled and nodded. "Mrs. Newberry, I don't mean to pry, but I'm curious about your walks to the cemetery."

Puzzled about how I knew her routine, she paused and looked down at the sidewalk before answering. "Christmas is nearly here, so I brought a wreath to place on my husband's grave this morning. We shared a love of Christmas, so no matter the weather, I honor him with a wreath."

"So, it's your husband you visit? How long has he been gone?"

"Three years, nine months, and three days. I miss him terribly, so I spend what time I can with him each day. He used to love watching me make quilts, so I take one with me when I visit him. He always wanted to see what I was working on."

"How sweet. Don't you get cold sitting out there?"

"Well, the quilt helps keep me warm. I can't wait to bring him flowers in the spring. The roses in the backyard were his favorites. He nursed them along for years."

"How wonderful. Thank you for sharing your story with me. Your husband was a lucky man to have such a devoted wife."

"He'd do the same for me. We were married for almost sixty years. I'll be right next to him again one day. Perhaps if you're still around, you'll pop over for a visit."

I didn't know what to say at first.

"I absolutely will," I said, nodding and smiling.

"I'm working on a small Christmas quilt for him. You may think that's strange, but it gives me great comfort to pay my respects. He always wanted to know the name of the pattern I was working on. Christmas quilts were his favorite."

I wanted to give her a hug, but I kept my place.

"I'd love to see that Christmas quilt when you're finished, Mrs. Newberry."

"You fancy quilts, do you?"

"Oh, yes. My mother and grandmother quilted. I wish I'd paid more attention to their work. I chose to spend my time writing instead of sewing."

"I bet you're quite good at writing. Well, thank you again for the cookies."

I went upstairs and tried to process what I'd just learned from her. She certainly was dedicated to her husband. I was glad I'd finally gotten up the nerve to ask her about her daily walks. I bet Mrs. Newberry wasn't the only one in this neighborhood who had an interesting story worth listening to and perhaps even worth writing about. I rarely saw other neighbors because they either left early or came home late. What did they do for a living? And do any of them also quilt in the cemetery?

The days passed. Most mornings, I'd hear Mrs. Newberry leave for her daily trip to see her husband. She'd be so bundled up for the cold that she could hardly walk. Why didn't she drive her car that was parked in the garage?

On Christmas morning, I was about to leave for church when I spotted a package in front of my door that was wrapped in vintage Christmas paper and topped with a handmade bow. I quickly ripped it open. Inside was a lap-size red-and-green patchwork Christmas quilt. The note enclosed read *Merry Christmas from Mr. and Mrs. Newberry. We hope it keeps you warm this Christmas season.*

This would be a Christmas to remember. One day I'd need to walk to the cemetery to thank Mr. Newberry.

Andi's Coffee Chocolate Chip Cookies

2 sticks butter, softened

¾ cup granulated sugar

¾ cup light brown sugar

1 tsp vanilla

2 eggs

2¼ cups all-purpose flour

¾ tsp baking soda

½ tsp kosher salt

1 tsp cinnamon

½ tsp instant coffee

16 ounces mixed chocolate chips
(I use one package dark and one package bittersweet)

Generous ¼ cup walnut pieces (optional)

1. Preheat the oven to 350° F.

2. In a mixing bowl, cream the butter and both sugars until fluffy.

3. Add the vanilla and stir until well mixed.

4. Add the eggs, one at a time, until well mixed.

5. In a separate bowl, mix the flour, baking soda, salt, cinnamon, and coffee.

6. Slowly add the flour mixture to the butter mixture.

7. When the batter is well mixed, add the chocolate chips and nuts, mixing well.

8. Form cookies using two soup spoons or tablespoons, and put them on a greased cookie sheet, spaced 1 inch apart.

9. Bake for 15 minutes or until done to your liking.

10. Remove from the oven and cool on a wire rack.

11. Repeat with the rest of the batter until all the batter is used. (You should get about 60 cookies.)

12. Store in an airtight container.

A "Home Alone" Christmas

I can see nothing but water, snow, and ice shoves building up along Lake Michigan. I'm sitting in my happy place: my lakefront log cabin. This cabin was a vacation home for generations, but now it's my permanent home.

The few acquaintances I've gotten to know have died or moved away. Some were snowbirds who were only here in the summer months. My cabin is in the woods, set back from the main road, so I don't even see passersby. My narrow gravel road dead-ends at the top of the hill where I live.

I know every nook and cranny of this cozy place. I can tell you when and where the sun sets and rises and what each storm sounds and feels like.

I'm now in my early seventies, and my only outings are to the local grocery, the gas station, and the mailbox at the end of the road. I don't like to refer to myself as a recluse, but I may have to admit that I qualify.

I'd sailed through the Thanksgiving holiday without feeling like I should have been somewhere else, but now Christmas was nearing. By all normal standards, I should be shopping and entertaining for the holiday ahead, but I was happier watching everyone else go through those motions. I quickly dismissed the thought of putting myself through either of those activities and parked myself in front of my large, stone fireplace that comforts me during the winter months. Add one or two of my favorite quilts to snuggle with, and I'm happy as can be.

I qualify as a quilter. I made quilts with gusto when I was younger, but now I just like to read about them and burrow beneath them. I've inherited several from relatives. I think of the maker each time I brush my hand along their tiny stitches. Sometimes I don't know who made a particular quilt and just try to imagine what the quilter may have been like. The antique quilts I have are my favorites. If only they could tell me their stories.

I pulled out some recipes pertaining to the season, including my grandmother's Christmas stollen and our family's delicious sugar cookies. The smell alone put me in a festive mood. Baking just for myself felt selfish, but it made me happy.

I knew I had mail to pick up from the post office, but I didn't want to walk through several inches of snow to retrieve it. The snow had been falling since yesterday after-noon and was really starting to pile up. A few Christmas cards had managed to find me before the storm, and I cherished the personal messages some included.

I wasn't much of a TV fan, but I did have a few favorite movies at my disposal, including *Pride and Prejudice* and *Casablanca*. Christmas movies also pulled me in. The original *A Christmas Carol* was my favorite.

The closer it got to Christmas, the more my childhood memories surfaced. Christmas Eve was the highlight when I was a young girl because it meant participating in the church's holiday programs. I love the smell of oranges to this day because my siblings and I each received an orange and a bag of hard candy after the service. Those small treats left a big impression.

One Christmas, when I was four, our cedar tree caught fire from the bubble lights that were so popular at the time. We had a houseful of people when the fire quickly spread to a nearby curtain. I screamed at the top of my lungs as my father bravely grabbed the tree with his bare hands and carried it out the front door. Thankfully, the fire didn't really damage the house.

I peeked out the window facing the lake and noticed that the snow was covering it now. The wind was fierce, creating a huge drift in front of the door. When there was this much snow, I imagined it as a warm blanket covering the yard. I did worry about snow accumulation on the roof. Years ago, I'd climb up and shovel it off, but I certainly wouldn't attempt that anymore.

When I awoke Christmas morning, the sun was shining bright, and every window glistened. It was like being in a crystal ball. I put on my robe and started my coffee, just as I did every day. I looked over at the strand of white Christmas lights above my mantel and then at the manger scene under the tree. Welcome, Christmas.

I turned on some Christmas music and thought of the baby Jesus being born this day so many years ago. What had the day been like in that cold, breezy stable?

After putting a couple more logs on the fire, I sat down to enjoy my Christmas stollen and coffee. When I finished, I made my way to the cedar chest and pulled out a scrappy quilt. It was heavier than the others in the chest and would surely keep me warm.

I arranged the quilt around me, enjoying its weight. Names were embroidered on it, which made me think it was a friendship quilt of some kind. I'd inherited it from my mom, who'd inherited it from her sister. Aunt Mae had told me once that this quilt had belonged to my grandmother and was made in the late 1800s. It remained in good condition despite its age. Mother was always afraid the red embroidery stitching would fade if we washed it, so we never used it.

Even though I didn't know those whose names were embroidered on the quilt, I took the time to read some of the messages about them. One block caught my eye: "Remember me, Francis B." Our family had a Francis who lived next door, so that message made me smile. Another read, "Roses are red, violets are blue. This is from your cousin Sue." I had to chuckle, thinking how Sue was most likely young and fun when she quilted that. One block was an embroidered heart reading, "Your beloved Aunt Ethel." I knew there was an Ethel in our family tree. Another block reading, "Forget me not. E. K." had small, embroidered forget-me-nots beneath it. I loved that one.

One block was "Mary loves Rudy." Was Mary single when she made this? How did she know my grandmother? The more blocks I read, the more questions I had. I really couldn't assume my grandmother made the quilt just because it had been hers. Only one block was dated, and it said, "Alice, 1899." Was that the year she signed it, or was Alice the maker who finished it in 1899? It dawned on me then that my grandmother's full name was Mary Alice Schnarr. Perhaps she used to go by the name of Alice. Oh, I hoped the Alice in the quilt was her.

Hours passed as I visited with each block. I was snowed in and by myself today, but this quilt made me feel like family and friends surrounded me. Occasionally, I pulled the fabric up around my neck and imagined that the folks who sewed it were offering me a hug. Did they know how much their words would mean to me all these years later? I felt their presence as if they were right here in front of the fireplace with me.

I was home alone, but this was one of the best Christmases ever.

THE ART OF THE SNOWFLAKE

I look to the sky to greet them as they fall on me.
Such intricate designs, and no two are alike.
I quickly admire each one, taking care not to disturb them.

Each flake, eager to join the others that have accumulated before it,
brings us pleasure, beauty, and the silent peace of winter.

The Christmas Button Jar

Everyone has a jar or some other means of storing their extra buttons. I know this because I grew up with Aunt Betty, who had a button shop.

Aunt Betty took care of me a lot growing up while Mom worked as a server. Mom appreciated my aunt's generosity because, as a single parent, she was counting on every penny to get by.

When I was six, Aunt Betty kept me busy in the back room of her shop sorting buttons by their color. As I grew older, the sorting became more involved. If I had a pile of red buttons, which were my favorite, she would tell me to separate the glass ones from the plastic and the cloth-covered ones. I was learning the tricks of her trade. She said that each button was like miniature art and that no two were alike.

A curtain separated the back room, where I did the sorting, from the customers out front. She told me to stay in the back, but every so often funny-sounding voices or stories got the better of me, and I'd peek through the curtain.

Customers would bring in or talk about the button jar their family had been holding onto. Aunt Betty would examine their jars and listen to their stories before paying for the contents.

After they left, Aunt Betty would bring the latest jar to the back room and decide whether the buttons were ready for sorting in a pie tin or whether they needed to be washed first. Only Aunt Betty would wash them; she didn't want to lose any to the drain.

She informed me that you could tell a lot about a family just by observing the buttons in their jar. Military buttons, fancy dress buttons, and utilitarian buttons for clothing all told different stories about family history. Sometimes the button jars contained other things like hairpins, garters, and pennies. We had some good laughs about the items we found.

Aunt Betty always reminded me that she had a special jar set aside for Christmas buttons. It was her personal favorite. I always hoped I could find one of those to make her happy.

When Aunt Betty wasn't busy with customers, she was sewing on buttons for people or creating merchandise for the shop to sell, like button jewelry. She occasionally had to arrange the boxes of buttons that lined the walls of the shop. The walls were labeled by their button category. This was especially important for the button collectors who visited frequently. Aunt Betty also called collectors if something came through that she knew they'd be interested in. They appreciated those calls and got pretty excited sometimes.

Even when I was in high school, I still stopped by the shop on my way home. I felt personal ties to the shop from all my time there over the years. I'd ask how busy she was that day and if she'd bought any new buttons. If she needed my help, I'd offer to stay even though I never was paid. She'd offer me a cup of hot chocolate or a cookie if she had them on hand.

One snowy afternoon, I noticed that Aunt Betty's closed sign was posted in the window even though her car was parked out front. I knocked on the door, and she let me in. She explained that with the severe weather she'd decided to close early. I followed her to the back room, which was always warm and cozy, and asked her what she was working on. She explained that with Christmas coming, she wanted to lay out all the Christmas buttons to see what she might do with them. Her face beamed as she explained how she was sorting them. I couldn't imagine her selling the Christmas buttons because she loved them so much.

"They're all so individually beautiful," she said with admiration. "I'm putting all the holly leaves here and the Christmas characters there. And just look at all these star buttons! These are a few from a dress I wore when I was little. I can almost remember wearing it. Oh, and I bet this one was on someone's Christmas stocking at some point and popped off. Which of these are your favorite, Anna?"

"I think I like all the shapes and colors of the stars," I said after some thought. "The shiny ones are really pretty."

"Well, if you have time, why don't you sort this new jar that seems to have quite a few stars in it? I have some fresh snickerdoodle cookies I baked last night that you can snack on if you want." My eyes widened with delight.

At five o'clock sharp, Aunt Betty was ready to go home. I was ready, too. I hugged her goodbye and told her I'd be back soon to help her.

With Christmas festivities and my after-school activities, nearly a week passed without my stopping by the shop. One day I came home and Mom was crying at the table. She said that Aunt Betty had suffered a sudden stroke and died quite suddenly at the button shop. As a seventeen-year-old, I tried to comprehend what had just happened to someone I loved so dearly. I'd never thought Aunt Betty or the shop would cease to exist. The funeral was a blur. Some of the customers from the shop considered her family and came to the funeral to share their treasured memories of her.

On Christmas Eve, I convinced Mom to let me go into the shop for the last time, and she reluctantly gave me the key. I had no idea what would become of the place. As I approached the shop I'd spent so much time in, I noticed the closed sign still hanging in the window.

I opened the door, and the bell rang as it always did to announce the arrival of customers. But other than that, the room was cold and silent. Where was my dear Aunt Betty?

Everything was still in place, and I half expected someone to greet me at any moment. I looked into her cash drawer; there was the usual fifty dollars that she kept there for the next day. She must have died after she performed her usual closing routine. Had no one been here since her death?

I slowly walked to the back room and burst into tears when I saw all of Aunt Betty's Christmas buttons still laid out on the table. The star buttons I had started putting into the mason jar were just as I left them. I knew something needed to be done with her Christmas buttons that were so special to her. Perhaps a small quilt or a framed picture would be nice. With every button, I could almost hear my aunt's voice. She had something to share about almost every button. Her touch was in each display.

When I reached the house, Mom was sitting in the living room with a look on her face I hadn't seen before. I thought she was waiting for me to tell her about my experience in the shop, so I began sharing every detail, with tears streaming down my face. Mom's expression changed to a pleasant smile.

"Honey, I'm so glad you shared your love of the button shop with Aunt Betty. I just found out she left the building and its contents to us. She left it for your future because you loved it so much."

I was stunned. Perhaps I didn't understand what Mom just said. I wasn't even out of high school yet.

"To me? What do you mean? How can I work in a button shop while I'm still in school?" Mom grinned and reminded me that I'd worked there all my life.

"I think my sister knew all along her shop would be yours someday. I'm sure it was her way of thanking you for all your interest and dedication. This Christmas gift is just like her. You and I can run the shop together until you can take charge by yourself. We'll remember her love of maintaining it and ask for help from her when we need it. Now you'll have your own stories to tell with all of Aunt Betty's buttons. Merry Christmas, Anna.

Orange Button Cookies

½ cup Land O Lakes butter, softened

⅓ cup granulated sugar

⅓ cup firmly packed brown sugar

1 egg

1 tbsp orange zest

1 tbsp orange juice

4 drops yellow food coloring

2 drops red food coloring

1¾ cups all-purpose flour

½ tsp baking powder

3 tbsp mini chocolate chips (for buttonhole decoration)

½ cup mini chocolate chips or white chocolate chips (for thread decoration)

½ tsp vegetable oil (for thread decoration)

1. In a mixing bowl, combine the butter and both sugars. Beat at medium speed until creamy, scraping the bowl often.

2. Add the egg, orange zest, orange juice, and food colorings. Continue beating until well mixed.

3. Add the flour and baking powder, and beat at low speed until well mixed.

4. Divide the dough in half, and shape each half into an 8-inch log on a lightly floured surface. Wrap each half in wax paper. Refrigerate 2–3 hours or until firm.

5. Preheat the oven to 400° F.

6. With a sharp knife, cut the logs into ¼-inch slices. Place the cookies 1 inch apart on an ungreased baking sheet. Place 4 mini chocolate chips upside-down onto each cookie to resemble buttonholes. Bake until the edges are lightly browned, about 6–7 minutes. Transfer to a cooling rack and cool completely.

7. Repeat with the rest of the batter until all the batter is used.

8. Place ½ cup of the mini chocolate chips and oil in a bowl. Microwave, stirring every 30 seconds, for 60–90 seconds or until melted.

9. Spoon the melted chocolate into a resealable plastic bag. Cut off one small corner of the bag, and pipe the chocolate onto the cookies in an X shape to connect the buttonholes.

10. Store the cookies in an airtight container.

Makes approximately 60 cookies.

Christmas on the Front Porch

~ 🌿 ~

Front porches played a key role in a certain South St. Louis neighborhood. They were the living rooms of everyone who resided in the brick row of identical houses.

With nothing but an alleyway between the houses, you could converse with neighbors on each side without having to leave your front porch.

Families gathered together to celebrate every occasion and holiday with elaborate decorations and fanfare. When a daughter married, there was cheering and toasting of the bride. When little Johnny was baptized, all were invited. When a family lost a loved one, they hung a black cloth above the front door, and all the neighbors would pay their respects. There were no secrets. Many were immigrants from Germany and still spoke the language.

At Christmas, the neighborhood was lit up like no other. Neighbors helped each other on ladders and strung lights up and down the street. Manger scenes were common, and Mary and Joseph stood right next to Santa and the snowmen. Poinsettias adorned statues of Mary.

I had a bird's-eye view of this neighborhood when I rented an upstairs apartment from Gottfried Meyer. It was one of the larger homes in the area. Even though I wasn't related to the Meyers, they witnessed my comings and goings like I was. They worried and cared for me like I was ten years old. At times I was bothered by that, but I knew they meant well.

Mrs. Grebing, who lived directly across the street from me, was an avid quilter. She spent many hours hand-piecing, embroidering, and quilting on her front porch. When she completed a quilt, we all knew about it. She held it up for everyone to see—including those who didn't know her and were just passing by.

Regardless of the season or the weather, Mrs. Grebing always had a quilt or two on the front porch. Those who came to sit on her swing snuggled beneath one she kept there. Another quilt rested on the white rocking chair nearby. And, of course, the one she was working on was always across her lap. In the cooler weather, she kept a quilt wrapped around her to serve as her makeshift coat. Her quilts were often the topic of conversation. Her work was careful and detailed.

Mrs. Grebing was especially proud of the Christmas quilts she made that looked so festive on her green porch swing. There was always one she was trying to complete so she could give it away on Christmas. She could easily recite who she'd given Christmas quilts to through the years. I couldn't help but wonder how much longer she'd be able to do that.

It was hard to find time to visit with Mrs. Grebing alone. I loved hearing her stories about growing up and the traditions she and her family had that were so different from my own. She was gracious with explaining her current quilting projects too. By watching Mrs. Grebing and asking lots of questions, I learned enough about quilting to try it myself. I had no doubts about what my first quilt would be. It had to be a Christmas quilt. Then I could sit with Mrs. Grebing on her porch and tell folks all about *my* quilt.

Portly Mr. Schmidt, who lived four houses down, played Santa Claus for the neighborhood. Word spread quickly about when he'd make his appearance so that all the children could be present. Mrs. Grebing served hot cider on her front porch for all who needed to warm up. Many others were happy to provide cookies and candy.

Neighbors loved to show off their baking skills with seasonal treats from their homeland. They baked stollen and apple strudel along with traditional Christmas cookies and divinity candy, and they generously shared their bounty with others nearby. Christmas carolers were rewarded with hot chocolate and cookies.

When Mr. Schmidt wasn't dressed as Santa, he played Christmas music from dawn till dusk. He was hard of hearing, and his music carried up and down the whole street. Most in the neighborhood enjoyed the music, but when the carolers were ready to sing, I could hear a couple yelling at him to turn down the music. Blaring those songs was just his way of adding to the Christmas spirit.

I knew I lived in a neighborhood like no other. I never saw anyone move away. If someone died, a younger family member took their place. I couldn't even imagine a stranger moving to our street. Those who lived here were tight.

There was nothing like Christmas on the front porch in that neighborhood. The refreshments were plentiful, and everyone was welcome to sit a spell.

A QUILTER'S CHRISTMAS EVE DREAM

I saw the Star of David pattern, having long admired that design.

I used a midnight color for the sky, for it was just what I had in mind.

The shepherds' field was a patchwork of green, brown, and gold.

I figured it would best represent the story I was told.

For the three wise men, I thought of silks against the dirt and sand.

*Just like the Crazy quilts I'd made before,
these were feather-stitched by hand.*

Joseph had a coat of many colors, but I chose just tan and gray.

As he hovered over Mary, his love was there to stay.

For the Blessed Mother Mary, I chose an indigo blue.

I wanted her to look at peace after all she'd been through.

Finally was the baby Jesus, lying in a wooden crib of old.

I chose a white wholecloth quilt, stitched heavily in gold.

If this quilt were not a dream, I'd forever give it care.

It would bring me all the joy that I'd happily share.

The Christmas Chain Letter

I grew up during the Great Depression. I was born in the forties, and I don't remember a day when my parents didn't talk about the challenging times from the previous decade. Living through the Depression was something my parents and their siblings never forgot. It touched them in innumerable ways, but one of them involved what they referred to as *chain letters.*

To my dad, Fritz Meyer, and his six older siblings, sending a chain letter didn't entail mailing the same document to twenty people to avoid some superstitious harm. By *chain letter,* they meant a letter that each sibling would add on to and circulate through the United States Postal Service. Long-distance phone calls were expensive, but stamps were cheap.

I loved the letters timed for the holidays the best. Christmas was always a big deal for the Meyer family. No matter where or what they were doing, communication prevailed. Because my dad was the youngest, the Christmas chain letter would originate with our family right after

Thanksgiving each year. My mom or dad would write a short letter and send it to Uncle Alvin, the next oldest sibling. Uncle Alvin then added to the letter and sent it on to the next oldest. The letter then progressed through the lineup of siblings until it reached the oldest. At that point, the first letter was removed. By Christmas Eve, everyone had been heard from.

When a letter arrived, my siblings and I gathered around the kitchen table to hear Mom or Dad read the latest news, which typically started with a weather report. I was able to picture in my mind everything that I heard. Occasionally there were bits of humor and sometimes a concerning health report. (I remember at the time wondering what consumption and hardening of the arteries meant.)

When I was young, our tree caught fire, and in one of the letters my dad shared how lucky we were. He omitted the part about severely burning his right arm as he carried the fiery tree out of our house.

All my dad's siblings were successful entrepreneurs, and the letters kept us informed of the latest news on that front. Uncle Alvin, a carpenter, built a lucrative business on the side as a taxidermist. As a child, I remember being scared to go to his house that was decorated with stuffed deer, ducks, and birds. In his letters, he shared the latest animal challenge he was experiencing, one of which involved having to return to the government an eagle he'd stuffed and kept. Uncle Rudy, the second oldest of the brothers, was a great singer who organized choirs at his church. He was also the unofficial social director of the family, performing introductions, offering prayers, and telling jokes at weddings and funerals. He was a religious sort and always closed his letter with a lengthy prayer.

Two sisters of note were Aunt Gussie and Aunt Mary. Aunt Gussie, whose given name was Augusta, was the wild child of the Meyer family. She believed in astrology and managed to make a business out of it. That must have been really far out at that time. She often cast predictions in her letters. My mom and dad brushed them off as silly notions, but Aunt Gussie had paying clients who valued her astrological leanings. Aunt Mary was a well-known tailor.

Despite the siblings' individual interests, they joined their business ventures into a company they called the Meyer Development Company. Dad and his siblings lived in different towns, so when the company needed a consensus to approve a business action, they voted by chain letter to approve or disapprove the action.

Years after both my parents had passed, I was given my family's chain letters. At first I had no interest in reading them since my parents were no longer alive, but as time went on, I became more curious. One Christmas I was feeling nostalgic and felt it was the right time to revisit the letters. Their generation had faded, but their letters, carefully tied with red ribbon, brought me comfort. Just seeing my mother's handwriting again felt like a hug.

I sat by the fireplace with my Christmas tree aglow, ready to see if I could learn something new about my family. The first one I opened was right after Grandpa Meyer had died. I'd never gotten to know him because he passed away before I was born. Grandpa had lived with my mom and dad at the time of his death. The family sent a chain letter with a vote on how much to spend on the casket. These seven siblings who were raised on a farm knew how to manage the business at hand, whether the business was personal or professional. I admired that.

Their greetings and wishes for each other were touching. My heart melted when Mom mentioned me, the last of her five children, being born. She referred to me as a "change-of-life baby." She mentioned that I was a surprise for them but that my siblings were delighted to have a little one around the house. She noted that I was named after both my grandmothers. They gave me the name Anna Louise, a name I certainly hadn't appreciated in my childhood.

Though the grammar and penmanship were imperfect, these letters kept the family together. Today's Christmas greetings are expressed through pretty pictures or emojis on social media; their impact and legacy aren't even close to these handwritten letters that were passed from mailbox to mailbox over the years. These chain letters will outlast me.

I hope this nostalgic memory I've shared might inspire you to communicate stories with your own family. Write your experiences and feelings on paper so that someone else can hold them ten, forty, or seventy years later. Your family will be glad you did!

The Written Word

~ ❦ ~

There's no better time of year for the written word than Christmas.

Despite the latest technology of Christmas greetings, there's still room for a handwritten word or two. A hand-written note can sometimes make all the difference in someone's life. Maybe you've kept notes or cards from family or friends sent long ago. I know I have.

The history of the old-fashioned Christmas card goes back to 1843, when John Callcott Horsley of the UK designed a card for Henry Cole. The first card designed in the United States was by Louis Prang, a Prussian immigrant, in 1874. He had a print shop in Boston.

Christmas cards have changed with the trends over the years. Their popularity has been declining since social media became the main line of communication between families and friends. Greetings through social media are cheaper, easier, and quicker to send, but they lack something that cards sent through the mail have. Sending an actual card to a loved one shows that you've taken the time, no matter how short your message, to connect personally.

Some people include a Christmas letter, a yearly report of their family, with their card. There's an art to making these letters interesting and fun to read instead of boastful and boring. Hallmark actually has some tips on different approaches to use, such as creating a top-ten list for the year, including snippets from each member of the family, keeping it funny, and sticking to a theme.

If you're not one to write your own letter, you can select a card with the sentimental words already in place but then add a personal note at the bottom. Pouring yourself a cup of coffee first may be an effective way to prime your muse. Remain quiet with your thoughts and feelings, and the words will begin to flow. Choose words that tell your reader they're special. Listen to your heart.

The beauty of the written word is that it's eternal. The recipient can pick up your card or letter to read again and again, as time permits. Your words can be a real gift to another. They cost nothing, yet they are priceless to the receiver and might even be kept through the ages.

Gift someone with your words this Christmas.

Christmas on Cottage Row

"Oh, Jan, of course I'll do it!" I exclaimed. "My mom isn't in town, and who *wouldn't* want to have a mini vacation on Cottage Row in beautiful Door County, Wisconsin?"

"Well, if you're sure," Jan responded. "I hated to ask you, but I really want to go home for Christmas this year. I told the Harrisons I would house-sit till March, but as long as I can have you watch the house for me while I'm gone, it'll be fine."

"So, what will I need to bring?"

"Not much. You'll find food and drinks galore at the house, except for fresh produce, but you can purchase that at Fish Creek Market nearby. It'll be colder than all get-out, so be prepared for that. I'll leave you as much information as I can. Just be sure you arrive there the week before Christmas. I'll text you the alarm code to get in the house. Oh, and I'd recommend using the gas fireplaces instead of the wood-burning one in the den."

"Okay, no problem. I feel I should do this for you for free because it'll be more like a vacation for me, but I do appreciate your cash offering."

As I hung up, I was both scared and excited. Never in my life did I think I'd reside in one of those big, fancy homes along the bay even for a short stay. The area was, indeed, beautiful. As a kid, we referred to it as "Rich Row." Cottage Row was part of the village of Fish Creek, my favorite one in Door County. The "row" was a quiet road that led to expensive homes nestled between a cliff and the water of Green Bay. The winding, hairpin road had a canopy of cedar trees that created a cozy tunnel with a side stone fence that dated back a century or more. I'll never forget the first time I saw it as a child. It reminded me of something out of a storybook.

Cottage Row was known to have housed some famous people over the years, including Curly Lambeau, founder of the Green Bay Packers. He moved into a lavish home on the north end of the row in the 1950s. Homes on that stretch rarely left the family. Occasionally, one would fall into disrepair, and the owner would tear it down and build a new one in its place. The Harrisons' house was built in the 1880s, so I was most eager to see it.

Once it was time to go, I packed minimally. Jan had told me I could easily get snowed in for days, so I tucked the current book I was reading for my book club into my suitcase. Because the houses were down the cliff on the shoreline, there would be a challenge ahead if I chose to brave any harsh weather.

Jan told me the Harrisons' house was about nine houses down the row on the right. I also had their house number. My eyes widened when I saw their massive, historic home.

They had a curved, concrete drive that took me down to their three-car garage. I couldn't imagine driving up this hill with snow on the ground. I felt as if I were trespassing as I parked my car and approached the side door. Following Jan's instructions, I entered the code, and the door unlocked. So far, so good.

As I walked into the kitchen, my eyes were drawn to the red countertops and accents. I'd always had an appreciation for red, so this alone would bring delight to my days here.

Before I brought in my things, I decided to scout out the entire house. I slowly walked from room to room, wondering if I could find my way back to the kitchen. Jan told me she always slept in the green room upstairs, so I meandered about until I found it. Entering the green room felt like walking through a garden. Holly leaf wallpaper on one wall complemented the white wicker furniture and bed linens. How could I possibly disturb the white eyelet spread when it was time for bed? The room also had a small balcony that faced the bay.

After a while, I brought in my things and tried to make myself at home in my new bedroom. When I returned downstairs, I made sure I knew where to turn on the lights since it was getting dark. Then I peeked out the windows and noticed a huge patio that was well lit for security purposes.

I was starting to get hungry and wondered if I should have picked up a sandwich before settling in. Remembering Jan's words, I opened the upright freezer and discovered an assortment of interesting options. I chose a frozen lasagna dinner. I also saw a treat that Door County was famous for: cherry pie! The Harrisons had a broad selection of wine both in the basement cellar and in the kitchen. I selected a bottle of merlot, which was my standby. I was sure it would last the duration of my short visit.

I opened the first cabinet to find a plate for my meal and was delighted to discover white dishes trimmed in red. My experience thus far at the Harrisons felt like I was playing house. I giggled at the thought.

After dinner, I retired early to my room so I could reply to some emails and texts and call Jan about my safe arrival. She listened to me rave about everything before she responded. "I know how you feel! It will get even better, I promise. Enjoy every moment!"

Once we hung up, I dressed for bed. I felt a pang of loneliness at the thought of occupying this large house all alone at Christmastime, but I promised myself I'd heed Jan's advice and make the best of every day. Before turning in, I decided to catch the weather on the TV hanging on the opposite wall from the bed. I learned that a light snow would be falling nearly every day, just like in Green Bay.

I turned off the TV and reminded myself that I was safe here. I slipped under the heavenly sheets and was out in no time.

Morning brought with it a ray of sunshine on my bed. After my restful slumber, I had to rethink where I was. Ah, yes, Fish Creek. It was chilly, so I grabbed my robe and made my way to the kitchen where I knew there was a red Keurig coffee maker waiting for me.

To my surprise, I could smell coffee as I descended the stairs. How could that be? I looked over at the coffee pot, which was full of coffee ready for me to pour. The pot must have been on some kind of timer.

I took my coffee and toast outside to the nearby sun-porch. The view was incredible. Jan had told me she enjoyed the nightly sunsets when she'd house-sit. On one of the end tables was a book called *For the Love of Door County*, written by a local historian. I sat down to thumb through it and found a section on Cottage Row. Besides the history of the cherry orchards, I read a story about Mrs. Van Schroeder, one of the earlier residents of Cottage Row who always wore a red-and-white checked dress with a big hat and white gloves. She'd pedal her bicycle down to the Summertime Gift Shop in Fish Creek to retrieve a newspaper and a vanilla ice cream cone almost every day. She'd take a few licks of her ice cream cone before putting the newspaper in her basket to ride home.

I went inside and continued reading about many of the earlier settlers and how Fish Creek got its name from the Native Americans because of the good fishing in the area. Asa Thorpe settled in Fish Creek in 1855 with his relatives. His family started the lumber business and built a pier. I liked learning about this village that I was lucky enough to stay in for a while. Over the next few days, I flipped through some of the other books I found in the library on the first floor of the house.

I didn't contact Jan again until I heard the prediction of a big snowstorm coming to the county. Per her suggestion, I stopped at the Fish Creek Market to buy some produce and lucked into some brisket stew the owner had just made for takeout. I was tempted to add cherry cobbler to my cart, but I reconsidered because of the pies in the Harrisons' freezer. Jan also told me to pick up the Harrisons' mail from the post office on Main Street. It felt odd picking up someone else's mail.

With my errands complete, I was ready to head back. In the brief time I was gone, a light dusting of snow had fallen. Because of the impending storm, Jan had recommended that I park on one of the designated side streets nearby instead of in the driveway. I parked my car at the bottom of the hill where I could keep an eye on it.

When I walked inside the entryway, something felt different. I learned what it was once I reached the nearby den and noticed the gas fireplace had been turned on. That seemed odd. Maybe I'd flipped that switch when I was trying to turn on a light. I shrugged my shoulders and began to unpack my goodies for the snow-in.

I poured a glass of wine and made my way back to the warm fireplace, jumping when I heard lovely Christmas music coming from somewhere. Should I call Jan? I hated to disrupt her nice vacation, but something was off. The experience of this morning's brewed coffee, the fire in the fireplace, and the Christmas music playing didn't feel scary, just weird. I wondered if she'd experienced anything similar when she'd stayed here.

I dozed off near the fire in a big comfy armchair and didn't wake up until three thirty in the morning. The music had stopped, but the fire was still going. Half asleep, I found my way upstairs to the bedroom. In a fog, I undressed. My bed had already been turned down, as you might experience in a five-star hotel. Once again, I was too tired to think about the strangeness of it and slipped into a slumber.

I awoke at eight thirty the next morning when my phone rang. Jan was calling to check in on me. I wasn't quite awake, but I began telling her of my odd experiences. I told her I was fine, but I was concerned about the snowstorm.

"I thought of you when I saw the weather report. You know today is Christmas Eve, don't you? There's so much excitement here with the little kids that I almost envy your being there at the Harrisons' house all alone. Do you have what you need for tomorrow?"

"Yes, I picked up some food at the Fish Creek Market you told me about. I love that place! If I'm feeling ambitious tomorrow, I might bake one of the cherry pies in the freezer."

"Well, if you decide you want to cook, there's plenty of food available in the pantry and freezer."

"I'm on vacation," I answered. "I don't want to cook or clean up anything!"

Jan chuckled. "Okay. Well, I love you and wish you a merry Christmas. Call me if you have any questions."

"Merry Christmas to you as well," I said. "I have a feeling this will be a Christmas like no other!"

I hung up feeling determined to make the best of my little Christmas on Cottage Row.

I couldn't resist checking the front windows and then the back to watch the snow accumulating. The white blanket was gorgeous, and I could only hope to stay warm and dry.

The thunder and lightning outside made me nervous, so I abandoned my plans to make calls wishing everyone a merry Christmas. I could certainly understand why residents of Door County became snowbirds in the wintertime.

I poured myself some wine and took a stroll to study the lovely paintings and photographs that were on display in the hallway and massive living room. I was starting to relax when I heard a loud crash in the den. Alarmed, I ran to see what it was. The large portrait above the fireplace had fallen down, knocking down a lamp in the process. Luckily, the picture had landed in a nearby cushioned chair, so it seemed to be okay. The glass in the frame was still intact, thankfully. I'd have to tell Jan about this. I'd never be able to rehang this large frame by myself.

I returned the lamp to its upright position and then heard a noise coming from the living room. I rushed down the hall, but it took me a while to discover where the noise had originated. I scanned the room, and that's when I noticed that all the photos had fallen over on the fireplace mantle. One of them had landed on the floor and the glass had cracked. How in the world would I explain this? Most of the pictures were of someone's wedding. The one that had fallen to the floor was of the same woman who was in the large portrait in the den. I didn't know who she was. All I could do was put the pictures back in their place and explain things to Jan later. Perhaps the vibration of the thunder had caused this to happen.

I heated up some soup for a quick dinner and headed to bed. Today had been exhausting. *Some Christmas this was going to be,* I thought. I pulled the covers over my head to block out the noises from the storm. Within about 15 minutes, I dozed off.

Waking up the next morning, I wished myself merry Christmas. I thought of my loved ones and decided to call some of them to check in. I put on my robe, wondering what the rest of the day would be like. Had Santa visited during the night?

The bright sun was streaming through the kitchen window, and my coffee was once again waiting for me.

This part of my stay was pretty nice even though I couldn't explain it. I put some frozen muffins in the oven and then glanced outside to the patio off the kitchen. There stood a small pine tree, which I knew for certain hadn't been there before. It was obvious someone had placed it there for me. I gave it a shake to remove some of the snow before bringing it inside. After all, it was Christmas, and someone thought I needed this. Perhaps a nice neighbor knew I was here.

The tree stood about four feet tall and mounted perfectly on a stand I found in the garage. I placed it in the corner of the kitchen in case it still dripped moisture from the snow. The smell was divine. It truly was starting to feel like Christmas.

I had just sat down to eat my muffin when Jan called to wish me a merry Christmas. I caught her up on everything that had happened since our call yesterday. She listened carefully without interruption until I was finished.

"What do you make of this, Jan?" I finally asked.

"I was afraid to tell you about Claudia," she said shyly.

"Who's Claudia?"

"Claudia and her husband lived in this house for many years before her husband had an affair. Claudia moved out after that, they quickly divorced, and then he married his mistress. Claudia's spirit remained even after her death."

"So, the current Mrs. Harrison that you work for isn't Claudia?" I asked.

"No, she's been married to Mr. Harrison for quite a few years. Now, most of what I hear about the Harrisons is from their aides who come and go around the house."

"Is the large portrait in the den of Mrs. Harrison? Whoever it is is quite beautiful."

"Yes, that's her," she confirmed, and my heart sank. "It's not the first time that portrait has fallen. Other things have happened to show Claudia's dislike of the new Mrs. Harrison."

"Jan, this is kind of spooky!"

"I know it is," she consoled. "I see things all the time when I'm there, but I didn't want to frighten you by telling you about them before you agreed to stay there. It helps if you talk to Claudia and recognize her presence. Just explain to her that you understand."

"Really? Talk to a ghost?" I questioned.

"Yes. Try it. You're not in any danger. Just enjoy your Christmas and especially that tree."

I hung up with the strangest feeling. How could Jan leave me in this house with Claudia? I had to think this through.

"Well, it's nice to meet you, Claudia," I said aloud. "Thanks for not scaring me any worse than you have. I understand how you must feel about another woman taking over your lovely house."

After I said those words, I felt a sense of relief and climbed the stairs to dress. As I did so, Christmas music began playing. I smiled as I finished dressing. When I began putting on my makeup, I felt the urge to take things a step further. I took my red lipstick and wrote, "Merry Christmas, Claudia" on the mirror.

When I returned downstairs, I sat by the fireplace and began my Christmas calls. Those I told about my experiences were envious of my situation. I hung up feeling quite fortunate.

I strolled to the kitchen to heat up my turkey and smelled the aroma of a cherry pie baking. Someone was being truly kind to me. To complete my Christmas meal, I decided to cook some boxed stuffing to accompany my turkey and pie. I went to pull the box from the cabinet and noticed that my tree from Claudia now had white sparkling lights. She was here with me for sure! I shook my head in disbelief. I was pretty convinced I'd lost my mind. Maybe everything would make sense later.

"Thank you, Claudia," I responded with a shaky voice. "The tree is so pretty, and I'd planned at some point to make that pie. You really didn't have to go to all this trouble."

As I prepared my meal, I felt Claudia's presence, so I said a few more things to her as I enjoyed my Christmas dinner. My time here was ending, and I wanted it to be as pleasant for both of us as possible.

I took a nap in the afternoon, wondering if things would be different when I woke up. I wrapped up my day with a cup of hot chocolate and a call to my mom and Aunt Clara. I didn't tell them I'd spent it here with the deceased Mrs. Harrison. After all, I'd had a most pleasant day.

I decided to leave the tree lights on for the night. When I went to the bathroom to brush my teeth before bed, I found a greeting from Claudia. On the mirror, written in bright red lipstick, was, "Merry Christmas to you too."

This was a Christmas I'd never forget. I'd met a new friend named Claudia Harrison, but I didn't even know what she looked like. I'd be willing to bet that each one of these marvelous homes on the row had an interesting story or two to share if only someone were open to hearing them. I'd love to hear their stories someday, but for now, I was content with my own experience shared with Claudia. I had my doubts that anyone would believe me, but I knew the story to be true.

White Gull Inn's Cherry Pie

2½ cups flour

1¼ cups plus 1 tbsp sugar, divided

1 cup lard

4–5 tbsp ice water

4 cups pitted fresh or frozen tart Montmorency cherries

¼ tsp almond extract

1½ tsp cornstarch

1. Preheat the oven to 425° F.

2. To make the pastry, in a large bowl, combine the flour and 1 tablespoon of the sugar. Cut in the lard with a pastry blender until the dough begins to stick together. Add the ice water 1 tablespoon at a time and toss with a fork until all the flour is moistened and the pastry forms a slightly sticky ball. Divide the dough in half and pat into two rounds. On a lightly floured surface, roll the dough to 2 inches larger than the inverted 9-inch pie plate. Place one round on the bottom of the plate. Set aside the other round.

3. To make the filling, in a medium bowl, combine the cherries and almond extract. (If using frozen cherries, drain and use ¼ cup of the juice with the cherries and the extract.) In a separate bowl, stir together the remaining 1¼ cups of sugar and the cornstarch. Gently toss the sugar mixture into the cherries to combine.

4. Pour the filling over the prepared crust, and then cover with the top crust. Pinch the edges and seal; trim the excess dough. Cut several slits in the top crust to allow steam to escape. Bake until the crust is golden brown and the filling is bubbly, about 35–45 minutes.

Christmas Country Church Tour

If, like me, you're from East Perry County, Missouri, you're familiar with the small German towns there, some of which have fewer than three hundred people. The county's rolling hills are populated by churches of varying denominations. Maybe you've even experienced the self-guided church tour that's been occurring two days each December for the past seventeen years.

I was an adult when I took my first tour. At the time, I wondered how everyone could travel on the winding roads in the dead of winter, especially since the tour lasted well into the evening. You're dependent on the brochure map to get where you want to go. The church tour started out with just a handful of county churches, but it has grown to include three other counties and nearly forty churches. It's a challenge to visit all the churches in two days, so planning a strategy ahead of time is helpful.

It takes four hundred volunteers coming together to make your visit special. Most churches decorate a real tree and bring in fresh greenery. You'll enjoy live performances and see unique manger scenes. One even has a live nativity complete with a camel! The churches, all at least one hundred years old, showcase a range of architectures and styles, from simple one-room clapboard structures heated by wood stoves to an elaborate shrine with a painted, domed ceiling and marble and bronze statues.

Members take the time to tell the story and history of their church, which they're quite proud of. All have stories worth listening to. You can learn how and when these churches started and any obstacles they've faced along the way. You'll likely walk away with some literature you can read later or keep as a memento of your visit.

I recommend taking a seat in the front or back row of the churches because there's much to absorb and listen to. You don't want to rush your visit. God resides in each one of these places, and you can feel that when you take the time to be still.

As you prepare to leave each stop, you'll most likely be offered refreshments. Knowing that visitors are on a tight schedule to see as many churches as possible on the tour, sometimes the refreshments will be in the form of a to-go bag. I can assure you that whatever the churches are offering was made with love by their members.

One of the more unique stops on the tour is the Lutheran Heritage Center in Altenburg. The historic log cabin is on the grounds of the first Lutheran college. Inside the center are at least fifty themed and decorated trees for you to enjoy, besides some of their regular displays. Occasionally, Christmas quilts are hung on the walls as well. Because the museum opens in the morning, many people start their tour there before visiting the churches.

Another added venue is St. Joseph Catholic Church in Apple Creek. You'll want to take a few minutes to enjoy the sizable manger scene outside the church and walk the stations of the cross that lead you to a beautiful grotto. Just make sure to dress appropriately so you can take in all there is to see comfortably.

There's an opportunity to show your appreciation for this free tour by leaving a goodwill offering. What's so special about this offering is that at the end of the tour, all the churches split the proceeds. This demonstrates how the communities come together as one for this unique Christmas experience.

I've gone on the church tour multiple times, and it's never quite the same. At the end of the event, you'll ponder which church was your favorite and recall your most touching moment. Maybe you'll even encourage your friends and family to join you for next year's tour. It's a gift for yourself.

May God bless you, each and every one!

The Pen Pal Christmas

Few can say they kept a pen pal for twenty years. When my bestie, Cora Beth, and her husband, Mark, moved to Minnesota, it felt like she was moving to another country. Our last goodbye in person was dramatic, to say the least. We promised each other we'd write every Monday no matter what. At first, social media wasn't as popular as it is now, so we stuck to that game plan with few emails or texts.

Our husbands thought our letter ritual was hilarious, but we didn't care. It was especially hard to be away from my best friend on weekends. Neither of us traveled much, so a visit was out of the question. Our lifestyles were so different, which provided amusing fodder for our letters.

When Cora Beth left, she was pregnant with her first child, and her family continued to grow after they moved to the country. They took over Mark's father's farm, so her letters were filled with stories of feeding chickens, canning, and birthing babies. She was quite a good writer. Her descriptions of watching their children take their first steps, being a soccer mom, and even just providing lunch to the workers in the field were most interesting to read about. I also loved hearing about her pets on the farm: Mittens, the cat; Betsy, the bunny; and Harley, the dog.

She and I shared a love for Christmas and for collecting handkerchiefs. Both of our mothers had a collection they passed on to us. I loved Christmas handkerchiefs, and she loved anything with hearts and valentines. When we lived in the same town, we'd go to antique shops, flea markets, and malls on the weekends in search of linen treasures. We had a tradition of including a handkerchief with any greeting card we mailed each other.

We were good about taking photos and making prints to send with our letters. Some of those she'd send me I'd attach to my bulletin board, and some I'd frame.

We knew that whatever we wrote in our letters was just between us. We were intuitive about each other's thoughts and feelings since we'd known each other for so long. When one of her kids was sick or she worried about money, I felt her pain as if it were my own. We shared the good and bad of our lives until, all of a sudden, we didn't.

My openness about sharing everything with Cora Beth was challenged recently when I went for a mammogram and discovered I had stage 3 breast cancer. I was so frightened, but I didn't tell her my news. Then I learned that the cancer had spread into my lymph nodes. The diagnosis was like a death sentence that I could barely share with my husband, Steve, much less my bestie. I was in denial, in hopes the cancer would just disappear on its own.

The doctor didn't waste any time starting my treatments of chemo followed by radiation. I became so ill that writing to Cora Beth seemed nearly impossible. I did manage to write her about the weather and asked a lot of questions about her children. Reading about her life each week helped me escape into her world and away from my own.

One of Cora Beth's recent letters asked me some questions I'd been avoiding, like what was happening at my job. She was always interested in hearing about those I worked with. I answered by making up a few details.

Losing my hair was devastating. I felt I'd lost my womanhood and would never be attractive to anyone again. How could Cora Beth relate? One night when I couldn't sleep, I almost gave her a call in a moment of weakness, but I decided that would be cruel since she couldn't do anything about my struggles anyway, especially from so far away. I had to figure out how to cope on my own.

At Thanksgiving, I was supposed to send a card with a handkerchief like I always did, but I had none to mail her. I felt bad, but I just told her I'd had no luck finding one. I received a delightful handkerchief from her that had fall leaves on it. Some of her hankies smelled like her, but I was starting to lose my sense of smell and couldn't appreciate them.

I got through the rest of my chemo and then started radiation, which weakened me even more. Cora Beth's letters talked about getting ready for Christmas, and I felt like I might not see another holiday. My husband suggested that we put up an artificial tree this year to make it easier on me, but I insisted on another real one. Too bad I wouldn't be able to smell it.

I was rapidly losing weight. Normally this would have been good news to share with Cora Beth, but I was only losing weight because I was sick. Meanwhile, she was baking all kinds of Christmas cookies and wrote about her calamity in trying to make her first fruitcake. I responded with humor and offered to take it off her hands. I bragged about our cedar tree and recalled a few memories that the two of us shared from Christmases past. Since I was confined, my past was becoming my present.

Steve's behavior toward me became worrisome. I sensed that he knew something I didn't. Neither he nor my doctors offered me the same hope for the future as they had in the beginning.

I told Steve that I wanted to send Cora Beth something extra special for Christmas this year. Money was tight for her, and I wanted to give her something generous. She hated her cell phone, but replacing that would have been complicated. Instead, Steve picked out a good camera so she could take photos and videos of her family.

Despite feeling downright awful, I tried to go through the motions of the season. I said yes to invitations from others but then had to cancel them shortly afterward.

The week before Christmas, I anxiously awaited a gift from Cora Beth, but none arrived. The doctors wanted me to go back to the hospital before Christmas, but I declined. As a result, hospice entered my world. No one wants to hear that word, but I was told that they knew how to deal with my circumstances better than anyone. To Steve's credit, he no longer tried to sugarcoat my illness. He suggested that telling Cora Beth would do wonders for my attitude and my willingness to live. I disagreed, saying that it would spoil everything. I wanted things with her to stay the same as they had been all these years. He finally agreed to honor my wishes.

On Christmas Eve, I slept off and on from the medication. Steve told me that my friends and family had been calling and wanted to stop by. He even mentioned having some Christmas carolers at the door. At seven that evening, he propped me up to get me to eat a little food. I wanted to please him so badly, so I managed to eat a little.

At eight, I heard the doorbell ring. I ignored it till I heard a familiar voice: Cora Beth. I could hardly believe it. We hadn't seen each other in so long, and I knew I must have looked horrible. She looked surprisingly like her mother. She asked if I could hear her. I nodded, but everything was a bit foggy. My eyes filled with tears. My emotions were so jumbled.

"I decided it was time to deliver my Christmas present to you," she said as she took my hand. "I want you to get better. Do you hear me?"

"I'm sorry," I whispered softly. "How did you know?"

"I read between the lines, just as we've always done," she said, choking up. "I love you, my friend. I brought you the prettiest Christmas handkerchief I've ever seen."

She opened my palm and placed it in my hand. I could feel the softness of the fabric but felt too weak to open it enough to look at it.

"Thank you," I whispered. "I will take it with me."

I gripped it tightly until I fell into a deep sleep of contentment. I smiled, knowing Cora Beth and I were together and that we would meet up again one day, surrounded by our pretty handkerchiefs.

My Feather Tree

It wouldn't be Christmas without both the chore and the joy of owning a feather tree. I enjoy them, but not everyone shares my sentiments. Inherited feather trees are most likely old, sparse, and showing some wear, just as all of us do once we reach a certain age.

Feather trees have an interesting history. When I've explained the trees' history to those who have asked me why I like them or given me a strange look when they've seen mine, their perspective softens. Just in case you're not familiar with the story, I thought I'd share it with you too.

Feather trees originated in Germany in the late 1800s and are considered the first artificial Christmas trees. Teddy Roosevelt helped popularize them in the United States when he was president. To promote conservation, he declared that the White House would use no live trees. By the 1920s, many department stores in the States began selling them.

The dyed goose feathers of these trees are wrapped around and attached to wire branches on the tree's trunk.

The wires, which bend to make storage easy, are fragile and sometimes break. The trees range in size from 2 to 98 inches. Most are green, but some are white to represent the white pines in the German forests.

Because these trees originated in the 1800s, they needed to accommodate lit candles. Many trees came with metal candleholders already attached to the generously spaced branches. Traditionally, the candles were lit only on Christmas Eve and were carefully attended. Some manufacturers attached a red plastic berry at the end of the branches.

The large spaces between branches allows room for elaborate ornament collections. When it's time to decorate my tree, I revisit every ornament. Some of them are homemade and quite primitive. When I finish decorating, I either wrap white cotton under the tree to represent snow or assemble a tiny, wooden fence around the tree; many trees come with a fence. I also enjoy displaying an antique Christmas quilt beneath my tree. I've seen others set up antique manger scenes or villages under their trees to add to the tree's story. When I'm finished decorating, I stand back and again admire the tree's primitive beauty.

Most people store their tree covered, without its ornaments, in a temperature-controlled closet. You should never store it in an airtight container.

These marvelous trees are a wonderful part of our past. I hope that hearing the history of feather trees has helped you appreciate their unique beauty.

CHRISTMAS FAVORITES

My favorite TASTE of Christmas is a sip of peppermint tea.

I also like candied stollen, but that's the German in me.

My favorite TIME at Christmas is seeing all my family.

I also like shopping when some of it's for me.

My favorite SMELL at Christmas is our fragrant cedar tree.

I also like fresh cookies in all kinds and shapes to see.

My favorite Christmas TRADITION is the carols that we hear.

I also like to be at church, where I know my God is near.

If you know your FAVORITES at this special time of year

Enjoy them to the fullest as I wish you Christmas cheer!

EAT CAKE

If you feel stressed about Christmas coming, EAT CAKE.

If the cold weather frightens you, EAT CAKE.

If the thought of shopping tires you, EAT CAKE.

If you hate making Christmas cookies, EAT CAKE.

If Christmas music annoys you, EAT CAKE.

If you have to ignore your family to be happy, EAT CAKE.

If Santa doesn't make it to your house, EAT CAKE.

If you've chosen not to do a gift exchange, EAT CAKE.

If your children or others become naughty, EAT CAKE.

If you get unexpected company, EAT CAKE.

If you're given an unwanted fruitcake, EAT CAKE.

If your bills are higher than expected, EAT CAKE.

If Christmas Eve has left you helpless, EAT CAKE.

If it's now Christmas morning, EAT CAKE AND CELEBRATE!

Those Bells

Nora Richard complained regularly about the bells that rang loudly and frequently across the street at Mt. Hope Presbyterian Church. When she moved into her upstairs apartment in a quaint neighborhood, she thought it most charming to live across the street from the historic church. She didn't attend the church, but she appreciated the excellent care given to the grounds.

It didn't take her long to notice that the bells rang not only to announce every church service, but on the hour. Neighbors convinced her she'd get used to the bells and pay them no mind after a while.

Nora worked from home, so she was pretty secluded from the general public. She spent most of her time watching the world go by from her office window that faced the front of the church. She could describe who went in and out and what time they did it. There were times she felt she was living her life by observing others.

She witnessed funerals and weddings. Once she saw two funerals in one day: one in the morning and one in the afternoon. Witnessing the grief on the faces of the families got to her sometimes, and she'd have to look away. She much preferred the gaiety of the weddings happening across the street. She loved seeing the dresses of the brides and the bridesmaids and watching the couple exit the church, hand in hand, just married.

At fifty, Nora was single and had never been married. She'd had brief relationships, but they'd never gotten serious. And at this stage in her life, no one was asking her to be a bridesmaid either.

Nora took an early morning walk every day around seven o'clock, with the bells chiming in the background. She'd been noticing a handsome man, about her age, who sat on a bench near the church. She assumed he worked at the church in some capacity because at eight o'clock every day, he'd make his way inside the office there.

Their encounters were never more than a few words of "Good morning" and perhaps an observation about the weather. He soon figured out that she lived in the apartment across the street and occasionally remarked about something going on in the neighborhood. His eyes were intense. She blushed every time he spoke to her.

One morning, the man on the bench actually asked what her name was and where she worked. She responded awkwardly, but her shyness kept her from asking him any questions about himself.

A month later, Nora tripped and fell near where the man was sitting. He rushed to rescue her and encouraged her to sit on the bench to compose herself. Nora was embarrassed, but she followed his advice. After they assessed there was nothing seriously wrong, he insisted on helping her up the stairs to her apartment. Her knee felt sore, so she didn't refuse his offer.

Nora invited him in for a cup of hot tea since he'd been so kind. They sat around her modest kitchen table as she nervously prepared some Earl Grey. This gave her an opportunity to ask him where he worked. It turned out that was a counselor for the church and taught classes there every morning at eight o'clock. He enjoyed sitting on the bench to plan his day while taking in the view of the beautiful grounds and listening to the bells.

It was nearing time for his class, so she knew he couldn't stay much longer. Before he left, he asked again how she was feeling. She told him she felt better and then nervously asked his name. It was Keith Kohl. Nora thanked him over and over again for helping her into the house. He just grinned and nodded.

She watched him cross the street. It had been a while since she'd had a one-on-one conversation with a man who was attractive and interesting. She wondered why she didn't ask if he was married.

The next morning, Nora felt the effects of her fall and knew she wasn't up for a walk. That didn't stop her from peering out the window to see if Keith was sitting on the bench. At a quarter to eight, she saw him walking toward her apartment. Still in her robe, she rushed to comb her hair.

When she heard the knock, she only opened it as far as the chain lock would let her. Keith gave a wave when she opened the door and asked if she was okay. She reported slight pain and told him she thought she should rest today. He agreed and said he hoped he'd see her tomorrow. Her heart melted at his kind words. Nora knew, no matter the pain, she was going to walk tomorrow morning.

Nora did, indeed, walk the next day, despite her minor discomfort. Afterward, she joined Keith on the bench for a short while, and their conversation was more extensive. He eventually revealed that he'd never been married. She felt a sigh of relief.

One Friday morning Keith asked her if she'd go to a movie with him that evening. Nora couldn't believe he'd asked her out, and she eagerly accepted. It had been years since she'd been on an actual date. The rest of the afternoon, she pondered what she should wear and what she should say.

The drive to the theater was awkward, with Keith doing most of the talking. He said he was surprised she didn't attend the church since it was so close by. While she was trying to think of a reply to that, he moved on to another topic. Fortunately, she didn't have to think of anything to talk about during the two-hour movie. She was so new at this. When it was time to drop her off afterward, he walked her to the door to say goodnight. She was too timid to ask him in, thinking he'd be relieved that the night was over and just wanted to go home.

That evening, the church bells kept Nora up all night, giving her plenty of time to replay her first date in ten years. She liked the movie, and she liked Keith. But she was afraid to think of him too fondly because she was certain he thought of her as just a friend.

The following Monday morning when she looked out her window, she saw no sign of Keith. She knew he lived in the neighborhood, but she had no contact information for him. Days went by, and her concern grew. She was almost tempted to contact the church office and ask about him. She wondered if he'd been fired or hurt, or if he just didn't want to run into her. At odd hours, she found herself going to the window to look for him. She began to feel very foolish.

The church bells were becoming more irritating to her as the days lingered on. Keith had expressed how much he liked them, so now they were just an unpleasant reminder of him. Did she just imagine the brief time they'd spent together? She didn't even enjoy the weddings across the street now. They made her feel jealous and unloved.

One Sunday morning about four weeks later, Nora glanced out the window out of habit. This time she did a double take. Keith was walking her way! A few minutes later, he was at the door. He was wearing a big grin and asked if she would welcome in a stranger. Nora jumped into action, confused about why he was there after such a long absence but happy to see him nonetheless. When they were settled at the table, Keith told her that his brother had died suddenly in Ontario, Canada, where he was from. He was apologetic about not contacting her, and she could feel her body relax. Nora offered him a hot breakfast of pancakes and bacon, which he eagerly accepted. Hours passed, as did several cups of coffee, as they learned more about each other. There was no awkwardness today. The conversation flowed easily.

The two of them began spending time together almost every day. Often it was just a walk around the neighborhood, but they did other things too. She loved the surprise he planned one Saturday. He called and told her he'd pick her up in twenty minutes for a fun adventure. They ended up going for a scenic drive to see the fall foliage, having a picnic under a canopy of trees, and then riding horses at a state park. It was her first time riding, so she was timid at first, but once she got the hang of being on a horse, she really loved it.

They discovered that they both enjoyed cooking. Sometimes they'd make dinner for the other, but they found it fun to scour recipes online and then prepare them together. Keith learned that Nora didn't like mushrooms, and Nora learned that Keith had a sweet tooth.

The week before Christmas, while having dinner at Nora's apartment, Keith asked Nora if she'd attend church with him on Christmas Eve. He told her that the service would begin at five o'clock, but they should get there early because it would probably be crowded.

When the day arrived, Nora felt excited about what was to come. It would be her first time inside the church across the street. She decided to wear an emerald-green dress she had in the back of her closet. She hadn't worn it for a few years, but it still fit.

Keith arrived at twenty till four, and they walked over to the church together. Keith introduced her to the pastor, who welcomed her and told her he was happy she had joined them. The church was filling up, but they found a seat in the third row on the left side. Once seated, she could really take in the church's beauty for the first time. The ornate ceiling and stained-glass windows were breathtaking. As the service began, the bells began ringing. They sounded different inside the church than they had from her apartment. She found the bells lovely and comforting.

They came back to Nora's apartment after the service. She told Keith she had a gift for him, and he said he had one for her also. Nora poured them each a glass of wine and then sat next to him on the couch.

Just as she did, Keith took her by surprise and got down on one knee. Nora held her hand to her mouth, surprised at what was happening. He took some time before saying anything, but then he began. In a shaky voice, he told her that after being away from her when his brother died, he missed her, and these past several months made him realize that he never wanted to be apart from her again. He took her hand then and asked her if she would be so kind as to marry him.

She hadn't expected this at all and remained silent at first. They hadn't really known each other that long. He hadn't even told her he loved her yet. Weren't they rushing things? She did love all the time they'd spent together, and she'd missed him, too, when he'd been away. But were they ready?

Keith looked embarrassed that it was taking so long for her to give an answer. He was about to get up when she suddenly said yes. They both began crying and gave each other a long kiss. Then the church bells rang out. It was perfect timing for their celebration.

On their wedding day, three months later, the church bells rang longer and louder than ever before.

Christmas at La Bell's Bed-and-Breakfast

I had grand ideas about seeing my daughter in Colorado for Christmas and then flying on to see my good friend in St. Louis, who was fighting cancer. Getting out of Seattle, where I'd lived the past five years, wasn't an issue, but due to a storm, the plane was forced to land in Boise, Idaho. Even if I had a day or two delay, I should still be able to visit my daughter for Christmas. I just wouldn't get there as early as I'd hoped.

Staff at the customer service counter told everyone that all the hotels nearby were booked, and the storm didn't appear to be ending anytime soon. My frustration and sadness got the attention of one of the attendants. She told me about a B&B forty miles away where she thought I could get a room.

I had nothing to lose, so I called the B&B. They did have availability, so I informed them I'd be there as soon as I could. I called my daughter and friend about the storm-related delay and promised to keep them updated about later arrangements. Darned snow! I just prayed my Uber driver could deliver me safely with the current conditions of the roads.

I thought it best to keep my conversation with the driver to a minimum so he could concentrate on the task of driving. Watching the car in front of us sliding, I was thankful I wasn't behind the wheel. The snow was beautiful, but I preferred observing it from the comfort of my house to driving in it.

After more than an hour, the driver arrived at La Bell Bed-and-Breakfast. I realized I'd been holding my breath for most of the trip, so I let out a long exhale. Safe and sound. Now I could relax. I stepped out of the car and gave the place that would be my home for the night a once-over. The gingerbread-style house was framed by colorful Christmas lights, and I couldn't help but smile. Was I really going to be staying in this charming place?

Mrs. La Bell, who had a round face and welcoming smile, greeted me warmly as I walked past the cozy entry hall. I told her my name was Rose and expressed how grateful I was to be there as I handed her my credit card. As she began the transaction, I noticed her Christmas tree off to the right. It was massive, strung with white lights, and full of interesting ornaments. I couldn't take my eyes off of it and felt compelled to examine it closer.

"Does this tree have only bell ornaments?" I asked curiously as my eyes took in the seven-foot tree. Mrs. La Bell smiled and nodded.

"Yes, indeed," she answered proudly. "I've collected bells all my life because of my name. I really love Christmas and am constantly on the search for new bell decorations."

"Well, your tree is stunning," I complimented her. "I've never seen so many bell ornaments. And I don't see two that are alike!"

"I used to travel a lot, so these bells are from all over the world," she noted. "Also, as you can imagine, my guests know about my collection, so I've accumulated some that way. And you're right—they're all different. I put up the tree at Thanksgiving so as many guests as possible can enjoy the ornaments."

Before Mrs. La Bell took me to my room, she gave me a tour of the downstairs. The Christmas decorations were as elaborate as any I'd seen. Bells were on the doors, on the fireplace mantel, on pillows, and even on the mistletoe. I tried to recall whether I had any bells in my Christmas decor. I couldn't think of any.

It was now ten o'clock, so I accepted her cup of hot chamomile to take to my room. Even her china had small Christmas bells on it. I carefully sipped my tea when we got to the top of the stairs.

She unlocked my room, revealing a glorious bedroom that had its own Christmas tree. The headboard and wood-work were decked with greenery also. I'd only seen this done in Hallmark movies!

"This switch here will turn off all the lights," she instructed. "Get a good night's rest, and we'll see you at nine for breakfast in the dining room. You'll meet the other guests then."

"Thank you so much," I gushed. "I certainly wasn't expecting all this."

We said goodnight, and I tried to relax from the stressful day. I was exhausted physically and mentally. As I undressed, my eyes wandered around the room, taking in every detail. I climbed into bed, noticing that even my bedside clock was shaped like a bell. I giggled at the thought of my ears ringing in the morning. I turned off the light and fell asleep quickly. Before I knew it, morning had arrived.

I decided to call the airline first thing. With the steady stream of snow falling, I guess I shouldn't have been surprised to hear that nothing had changed. Carl, my late husband, always told me to just enjoy the moment and not stress over the details. He had a point. I was stranded, but this was a pleasant place for it.

The breakfast buffet table had a red-and-green plaid tablecloth that was adorned with holly and berries. Topping several red platters were an apple braid, a cherry pastry shaped like a candy cane, two bacon and Swiss quiches, and a colorful offering of melons, kiwi, and blackberries. Suddenly I was feeling hungry!

The dining room table was covered by a deep green cloth and had silver bells as the centerpiece. Based on their patina, they looked like they could have been in the family for generations. The table could seat ten. I chose a spot at the end and sat down.

The first guest I met was Ted Cummings. I nodded as he said good morning and took a seat next to me. He told me he was a writer and was delayed on his way to New York. He looked about my age and seemed warm and approachable. The next to arrive was a young couple, Michael and Elizabeth Sparks. They never took their eyes off each other as they joined us. They mentioned that they were on their way to Florida to see his parents for the holiday. The last to sit at the table was a young, handsome man named Matt

Sutter. He barely looked up from his phone to acknowledge any of us. I guess he wasn't used to having breakfast with others.

We engaged in small talk for the first twenty minutes of our meal. When the topic turned to Christmas, I surprised myself by admitting that I hadn't really been in the Christmas spirit to put up decorations since my husband Carl had died four years ago. I'd never said that out loud before, and here I was sharing it with people I'd just met. My words got everyone's attention. They looked at me with sympathetic eyes.

"You don't even get a tree?" Elizabeth asked in disbelief. I shook my head.

Ted said he rarely put up a tree anymore because of his travel schedule. He said he could write anywhere, so this place suited him well for the holidays. He could enjoy the decorations without putting in the work of decorating. Michael and Elizabeth shared a funny story about their cat knocking down their tree not once, but twice last year. Matt cracked a smile but never looked up from his phone.

The Sparks excused themselves soon afterward to retire to their room. I had nowhere to go and was relishing sitting at this beautiful table eating a leisurely breakfast for a change.

"My daughter will be most upset if I don't get there for Christmas," I admitted to the group.

"Well, I'll try to make everyone's stay as pleasant as possible," Mrs. La Bell assured all of us. "I don't normally provide meals beyond breakfast, but I'm making an exception. With the roads as treacherous as they are, no one needs to be out."

"Thanks so much," I responded. "Please don't go to any trouble.

Just then the Sparks came downstairs and announced that they were walking to the park nearby and might try to make a snowman. They invited us to join them but soon figured out from our reactions that they were on their own. *Oh, to be young and adventurous again,* I thought to myself. I remember making snowmen and snow angels the first winter Carl and I were married. Love brings out the best in us.

After breakfast, I wandered into a small study off the living room. The walls were lined with bookshelves, and there were magazines in a stand near one of the couches. Ted followed me and began asking me more questions about myself. Our conversation was light until he asked if all the Christmas decorations here at the B&B bothered me because of what I'd said during breakfast.

A bit surprised, I answered, "That's a good question. Actually, I'm enamored by the lovely decorations here. I haven't done any decorating for so long that it's refreshing to see these. More than anything, I think I feel guilty experiencing joy this time of year since my husband died a few days before Christmas."

"Oh, I'm so sorry," he said quickly.

"I was angry at first," I confessed. "I threw everything away that even looked like Christmas. We had so many plans, and just like that, he was gone. Why couldn't I go with him? Of course, time has helped, as they tell you, but with my daughter away, I never had a reason to rekindle the Christmas spirit."

"I understand," he responded with kindness.

"I have to say, if this place doesn't put me in the Christmas spirit, I'm a lost cause," I joked.

He laughed and nodded in agreement. We were quiet a minute before he spoke.

"Rose, I'd like to ask you a favor if you have the time. I drafted an article last week that I'm about to turn in. With your background, I'd love to have your honest reaction to it. It wouldn't take long to read."

It seemed a strange request, but what else did I have to do?

"Okay, I'd be happy to," I said. "I brought a new book with me that I haven't started, so I certainly have the time to help."

Ted was happy I'd said yes and told me he'd get it to me soon. I wondered what background of mine would be helpful to his article. I guess I'd find out soon enough. He left, and I stayed in the den and flipped through a couple magazines until it was time for lunch.

After I had some of Mrs. La Bell's delicious leek and potato soup, Ted brought the article to my door. I didn't ask him in but graciously accepted his manuscript.

I closed the door and made myself comfortable in the love seat by the window to watch the snow still piling up. I sipped my coffee and began reading, happy to have something to distract me from the weather.

It didn't take me long to realize why Ted wanted my perspective. The title was "Turning Grief into Productivity." I was barely a page into the article when tears began to flow down my cheeks. I could certainly relate to the emotions being expressed in what I was reading. I got up and walked around the room before I continued. Two hours later, the conclusion was pretty much as I suspected it would be. A nonprofit group had been formed in remembrance of the woman's death. I couldn't help but wonder whether Ted had a personal connection to the woman in this article. I'd ask him about that when I saw him tonight.

I'd never been to a B&B that offered cocktails, but Mrs. La Bell really went all out for her guests stuck here during storms. I showered and changed into something more attractive in time for the gathering at five thirty. Christmas music was playing, and the appetizers on the buffet table looked as if they could have been on the cover of *Bon Appétit* magazine. Ted was ahead of me in line.

"I liked the article very much, Ted," I said as I handed him the manuscript.

"Honestly, or are you just being kind?" he asked.

Mrs. La Bell filled my wine glass before I answered his question.

"It hit some sore spots for me, as you can imagine," I confessed. "I couldn't help but wonder if this was something personal to you?"

"It was my daughter," he responded quietly.

"That makes the article even more special," I told him.

I didn't have a chance to say more, as Mrs. La Bell had other plans for us. She told us to gather by the front door. When she opened it, six Christmas carolers strolled into the foyer, singing their hearts out. Their voices were loud and merry despite their shoulders being covered in snow. Without hesitation, we all joined in to sing. Even Matt started moving his lips in response. Ted was standing next to me, and our eyes met, as if we'd shared something very personal.

The next morning, Christmas Eve, I made another phone call to the airline. It took me a while to get through, but I was told once again that all flights had been canceled. The storm just wouldn't let up. I was beginning to realize that I might not be seeing my daughter for Christmas after all. I called her to tell her our visit would have to wait a little longer and not to worry about me. She was surprised when I told her I'd been having an enjoyable time here despite the delay.

After I hung up, I went down to breakfast of biscuits and gravy that Mrs. La Bell had prepared for us. They were delicious, but my favorite part was the homemade apple butter that reminded me of what my mom used to make. Loaded with cinnamon, it was absolutely delicious. She told us as we ate that if there was any last-minute shopping we needed to do, our only hope was Gibson's, a drug store on the next corner. She said she was sure Santa would come to the inn because we each had a stocking with our name on it hung from her mantel. She encouraged us to find gifts to put in each other's stockings for the next morning. I'd never had a stocking of my own. We were completely surprised and didn't know how to respond. Buying gifts for strangers was new for all of us.

"Well, I guess I'll be making a trip to Gibson's," Ted quipped. "Would you care to join me?"

I laughed and nodded. We grabbed our heavy coats and boots and headed out into the windy snow.

Gibson's Corner Drug Store was like no pharmacy I'd ever been in. I was used to larger chain stores, like Walgreens. But this small, charming place had everything from prescriptions to clothes to local coffee and honey. All that was missing was the kitchen sink. And they'd gone all out decorating the store for Christmas.

Ted and I separated as we tried to think of generic gifts for the other guests at the B&B. A candy cane or a chocolate Santa wouldn't be sufficient.

I settled on getting nice fine-lined writing pens for everyone. They came in assorted colors and included a gift box. I figured that even Matt had to write by hand now and then. All I needed was a red ribbon to tie to each one. I was tempted to get myself a set of pens as well.

When we returned, it was time for lunch. Mrs. La Bell had prepared chicken salad sandwiches, grapes, and a cucumber salad. I could get used to having someone fix meals for me. After lunch, I decided to relax in my room. A nap and some reading sounded nice.

It was hard to concentrate on my new book with the aroma wafting from downstairs. Mrs. La Bell had spent hours cooking her grandmother's pasta sauce, which was her tradition on Christmas Eve. Dinner was lasagna, garlic bread, salad, and red wine. It was better than I'd had in any restaurant. As we ate our meal, everyone made a toast to those who couldn't be with us.

As we sipped cocktails after our filling dinner, Mrs. La Bell asked Ted to read the Christmas story. I hadn't heard it since I'd read it to my daughter years ago. It brought back fond memories of when we were a family of three. This Christmas was certainly different from what I'd envisioned it being. The time I'd reserved with my daughter was now being spent with strangers. I felt nostalgic about days gone by, but I appreciated that those around me tonight were becoming my friends.

Christmas morning, the snow had finally stopped falling, and the day was bright and cheery. Everything glistened outdoors. It was a visual reminder that Christ had been born on this special day, and He was our light. I said aloud, as I did every day, "This is the day the Lord hath made. Let us rejoice and be glad in it."

I came downstairs and managed to fill the stockings before anyone else. Then the others arrived, and we greeted each other with a hug and "Merry Christmas." We knew this would likely be our last day together. We had come from diverse backgrounds and hadn't planned to spend Christmas together, but here we were, and it was okay.

Mrs. La Bell had arranged a scrumptious breakfast buffet, and she suggested we take our plates into the living room where we could open our stockings. The laughter and merriment were a nice start to our last day together.

It was fun to see what everyone had picked out for each other. Mrs. La Bell thoughtfully gave each of us a bell ornament to remember her by. Michael and Elizabeth gifted us with pretty soaps and sachets. Matt found Christmas-themed mouse pads and apologized for the silly notion. Ted gave us fuzzy earmuffs, which were the hit of the morning as we tried them on. All seemed pleased with their pen sets, so I was happy about that. Matt took a great photo of everyone and told us he'd send us all a copy.

A sudden knock on the door caught us off guard. Mrs. La Bell opened it, and in walked a happy, round Santa who looked like the owner of the drugstore we'd shopped at the day before. He bellowed out "Merry Christmas!" as he passed out large candy canes and warm hugs. Matt tried to snap a photo of each of us with jolly ol' St. Nick. What a fun Christmas morning!

By early afternoon, flights started opening up. The Sparks and Matt had the earliest departures. We exchanged a round of hugs as if we were family and told each other what a pleasant time we'd had together.

Ted and I both had flights that were leaving close to five o'clock, so we decided to share a cab back to the airport. We thanked Mrs. La Bell for the best Christmas ever and told her it was one we'd never forget. I think she was sad to see us go.

In the cab, Ted and I exchanged contact information. He touched my hand and said he'd really like to get to know me better. Without thinking, I bravely picked up his hand and kissed it. I thanked him for turning my grief into joy.

When we arrived at the airport and it was time to part ways, he gave me a big hug and a kiss on the cheek. I watched him walk away and then got in line to check in.

I'd just had the best Christmas in years. Was it all a dream? I had to think it was all meant to be, and I couldn't wait to share the stories about it with my daughter. My feelings of guilt and sadness had been replaced with joy and hope for the future. Truly, anything is possible.

WHO ARE SANTA'S HELPERS?

Santa can take many forms during the holidays. Do you recognize him in any of the following people who could be considered his helpers?

- The bell ringers who stand at the corner to collect for those less fortunate
- The salesperson who's friendly and helps you find the perfect gift
- The soup-kitchen workers who come in to serve the hungry
- Those who give to organizations like Toys for Tots
- The carolers who spend time in the cold singing Christmas carols
- The clergy who stay late or pray for those in need
- The single moms who do without so their children can have a good Christmas
- The mom or dad who stays up late assembling gifts
- All who give effortlessly so the unfortunate can have a better Christmas
- Those who offer their time to those who are lonely or hurting

Thank you to all who embrace the spirit of giving.

"The Girls"
Christmas Reunion

"The girls," as the five of us were referred to back in the 1960s, thought we had it all. We'd been besties all through high school and did pretty much everything together, from cheerleading to sleepovers. But all that changed after we graduated. Our parents had chosen different colleges or vocational schools for each of us, and we shed countless tears knowing we'd be separated. The real world was waiting for us, but we weren't necessarily ready for it.

Our first real get-together after college was at our tenth high school reunion. We had a lot to catch up on, and catch up we did. After we left the venue, we stood out in the parking lot for another hour.

Carole had always been the party girl of the bunch. She had started going to the community college but in no time became pregnant and married her high school sweetheart, Dave. Dave complied with every one of Carole's wishes in high school, and that hadn't really changed ten years later.

Pat had always been the petite and cute one whom the boys loved to flirt with. Her parents had sent her away to a girl's school for college, and she hated every minute of it. She found ways to rebel against them for putting her through that.

Susan had been awkward in high school. She told us she'd dropped out of college quickly and tried unsuccessfully to make a niche for herself doing some modeling.

Nancy hadn't moved away like the rest of us had. She'd married the town lawyer, and they had a magnificent home near the high school.

I'd always been the teacher's pet in school and had wanted to be a teacher for as long as I could remember. I caught them up on the fact that, after graduation from college, I began teaching English in the same small town where I met my husband.

Fast-forward to the fall of this year. Carole, always our social director, decided it would be fun to get the group together for a reunion in our hometown around Christmastime. None of us was getting any younger, after all. Pat was battling cancer, and we feared she wouldn't be around much longer. She told us she was determined to be with "the girls" once again.

Carole announced that we'd meet at the school's senior-high building so we could see how it had changed through the years. Nancy told us we could come over to her house afterward. I think she was eager to show off their large home.

As our reunion date neared, we wondered who would really show up. Each of us had health and family circumstances that could easily get in the way of our coming together. I, for one, wasn't going to miss it. We were in our seventies now and knew our lives were on the downward slope. This might be the last time all five of us would be together.

The square, in the center of town, was decorated for Christmas, and the Sweet Tooth Bakery was still there, making the same donuts they always had. The town had grown ever so slightly. There was never much to do at the square back in high school, and it didn't appear much had changed in that regard. My perspective on the size of the buildings had certainly changed over the years, though. Things looked much smaller today.

I was the first to arrive at the school. Come to think of it, I was always the first to arrive. One of the staff members who had offered to give us a tour greeted me. She introduced herself as Grace. I'm sure I looked really old to her, as she must have been all of twenty-five. The school looked a little different, but it smelled the same.

Carole arrived talking a mile a minute as usual. Her round, happy face had barely changed, showing just a few wrinkles. After we gave each other a big hug, we saw Pat. She walked slowly and deliberately and was so thin. She was wearing a wig that was similar to a style she'd had years ago. We hugged her gently and then asked Grace if she knew of a wheelchair we could borrow for Pat as we toured the school. Grace happily retrieved one from the office. Pat eased into the chair, and then Nancy and Susan joined us.

Our fivesome was now complete, and the tears of joy started to flow. We shared a group hug as we always used to. It was going to be a good day, and I was glad we were together.

Grace told us coffee and tea were available in the library if we wanted some. With our beverages in hand, she began the tour.

Once we started strolling the halls, the giggles and stories commenced. The janitor's closet was still in the same place it had been when Pat used to sneak in there to smoke. The gymnasium that used to seem so big now appeared half its size. We stayed there quite a while discussing our cheer-leading practices for all the team sports and those horrible uniforms we had to wear for gym class. Carole even remembered one of our old cheers and demonstrated it for us. What a hoot! After the gym, we moved on to the old library, which was now a science lab. We shared stories about Mrs. Huber, the library monitor. I could still see her silver hair and gentle smile. I'd always liked her.

We talked about which teachers were our favorites and which we couldn't stand. The last of them had passed away a couple years ago, which reminded us how old we really were. We compared notes about who we had crushes on back then, when we got in trouble, and what some of our old classmates were doing now. What one of us had forgotten, someone else could fill in. It was a real trip down memory lane. Grace smiled listening to us.

We were truly feeling like "the girls" again. We ended the tour with Grace and then linked arms as we walked toward the front door. In the parking lot, Nancy reminded us of her invitation for cocktails. We agreed that drinks sounded great and followed her to her house in our respective cars.

Nancy's place was just a few blocks from the school. It was a grand house for sure, and she gushed with pride showing us around. Her husband had decided to hang out with one of the grandkids today so we could have the house to ourselves. She warned him we might be there for a while! We were encouraged to help ourselves to the spread of sweet and salty treats on her buffet table in the dining room. While Nancy's son made our drinks, I got Pat situated in a high-back chair. Pat was having a good time, but I could sense her discomfort.

There was nothing like cocktails and large stuffed chairs around the fireplace to relax us. Dirty details and long-kept secrets began spilling into our conversations. We caught up on children, grandchildren, pets, and travels.

Pat finally shared her battle with lung cancer, and the room suddenly became somber. Through tears, she told us her life was ending soon. She expressed her regrets, mostly over things she'd never get to see or do. We shared in her tears while encouraging her to keep fighting. We also shared our own health issues and our joys and struggles with marriage, middle-age dating, and remarriage. Susan said she'd marry for a third time, but the rest of us agreed that one or two marriages were more than enough. Our easy chatter reminded me of all the talks we'd had when we were young and had sleepovers.

We sat around Nancy's large Christmas tree for a few hours. We exchanged small gifts, and Nancy's son took some photos of us with his phone. We reminisced about past Christmases we'd shared together. Some of us had been friends since grade school, so the stories went way, way back. It felt so good to be together again, laughing and crying, all these years later.

We didn't want the day to end, but we knew it must. Carole said she'd organize a reunion every year from now on. We all said a tearful goodbye to Pat, knowing this would probably be our last time to see her, hug her, and hear her stories. I told myself that even when Pat was no longer with us, we'd still get together and remember her. I cherished these lifelong friends even more today than I did when we were in school together. We'd changed, of course, but our friendship had stayed the course. What a blessing to reconnect.

Friends are forever, even if one passes on. We will always be "the girls" in our hearts, with memories and secrets that pertain only to us. If you're lucky to have a good friend or two, cherish them like no other. Sometimes remembering the past is our best present to ourselves at Christmas.

Polly's Peppermint Shop

Polly's Peppermint Shop was located on Main Street between Harry's Hardware and Little Elves Christmas Shop.

Polly, the owner, was a wisp of a woman who looked like she'd never touched anything sweet in her life. But she loved making cookies and candy, and as her neighbor, I benefited greatly from her talents. Her shop was new, but she'd worked for a competitive bakery across town for many years.

Polly loved anything red and white and displayed some of her color-themed collectibles in her shop. Sometimes customers added to her assortment. Her decor certainly fit the peppermint theme.

I knew Polly was operating on a shoestring budget. She was a divorced single mom with a strong urge to create, and she'd wagered all she had to open her shop. Polly had a kind and friendly heart. She gave a free cookie to every child who entered the shop, and she donated goodies freely to non-profits that needed her help for fundraising.

Customers loved entering the cozy shop with the red-and-white awning out front. Polly's Aunt Susan helped her bake at night several times a week. Her niece Kelly and I also assisted part-time. But Polly was there day and night.

Polly was about to have her first Christmas season since opening six months ago. It was time for her shop to shine!

Business had been steady, but her biggest challenge was space. She couldn't expand since she was locked between two popular shops. She had to turn down business at times to accommodate all her orders.

The Christmas festival was coming up, and Polly knew extra orders could be a challenge for her. She didn't want to disappoint anyone, so she'd been putting in extra hours for the past week.

I picked up a flyer at the post office advertising a Christmas cookie contest. The winner would receive $5,000! I got so excited and immediately brought Polly the flyer so she could enter.

She stared at the flyer and shook her head, much to my surprise.

"No, I don't think so," she answered. "Mrs. Olson stops in and brags about her cookies nearly every week. She told me her neighbors and family tell her all the time that she makes the best cookies they've ever had."

Mrs. Olson clearly didn't have confidence issues.

"Polly," I said, "Mrs. Olson is just a braggart, and it's not true anyway that her cookies are the best. Yours are, and I know you'd win if you entered the contest. It'll be good for business, too!"

"Listen," she argued, "I appreciate what you're doing, but this flyer is geared toward stay-at-home moms and grandmas, not people who own bakeries. Besides, I already make ten kinds of cookies and don't have time to come up with a new one for this silly contest."

The following week Polly told me that Harry had come in from the hardware store to announce he was moving to the new strip mall on the outskirts of town, where most of his customers were from.

"He was kind enough to offer me the space if you can believe it!"

"Polly, that's the best news I've heard in a while! This is your sign to expand the shop!"

"Oh, I wish, but I can't afford it. I'm just scraping by for rent in the small space I have now. If I bought Harry's side, I'd be bankrupt within a couple months."

"I know it feels impossible now, but you may never have this opportunity again. The $5,000 prize money is waiting for you to say yes. Think of it as your way to add more tables and a counter."

Her aunt overheard us and told Polly she'd be crazy not to try. Polly didn't want to hear another word about it, though, so I went home discouraged.

The next morning, I was scheduled for the early shift at the shop. When I walked in, Polly was covered from head to toe in flour and was sporting a big grin.

"Here, taste this," she said, offering me a warm cookie. "I came up with a new recipe, but something's missing. I'm hoping you can help me figure out what it needs."

I put down my purse and took a big bite. She was right. It was good, but it didn't leave me wanting more.

"How about adding some peppermint and a bit more chocolate?" I suggested. "Everyone loves your peppermint cake, so I'm sure peppermint would be delicious in your cookies. Pairing chocolate with peppermint is sure to be a winner."

Polly went to work mixing a new batch of cookies with the added ingredients while I managed the shop.

It was closing time, and I needed to be on my way to meet a friend for a seven o'clock movie. Polly had just put another batch of cookies in the oven and looked exhausted. I was proud of her determination. She didn't mention the cookie contest, but I was fairly sure that's why she was experimenting today.

When we came out of the theater, my phone alerted me to a text from Polly.

"Stop by after the movie. It's important."

My friend decided to join me, and we headed straight to Polly's shop. It smelled divine. I could see the excitement on Polly's face when she proudly proclaimed she'd found the perfect cookie.

We each quickly took a bite and closed our eyes as the bursts of flavor filled our mouths. My friend declared it the best cookie ever and loved the touch of peppermint. I agreed and told Polly it tasted like Christmas.

Polly, grinning from ear to ear, said, "Oh, you've made me so happy! I'm going to call these cookies Christmas Kringles."

"That's the perfect name, Polly," I said. "Don't forget that the festival is this weekend. You'll need to register for the contest as soon as possible."

"I'll do that tomorrow. Would you attend the festival with me? You're the reason I'm even entering this contest, and I'd love your support."

"I'd be honored. I know you'll win. Now, may I please have another cookie? I need to make sure the second one is as good as the first!"

Polly laughed and gave both of us a cookie to go.

The night before the festival, she was up most of the night figuring out the best way to present her cookies to the judges. She tried different arrangements but finally settled on using a white ceramic cake stand. The cookies were perched on a red-and-white peppermint ribbon encircled by holly and berries.

When we arrived at the festival, I did a little checking. Eighteen contestants had entered, and yes, Mrs. Olson was one of them. Polly was listed as number sixteen.

When the cookie tasting began, we watched the judges closely for their reactions. Their eyes told us which ones they liked and which ones they didn't. When they finished, I tried to reassure Polly. She was so nervous that she couldn't stop biting her nails.

When the festival chairperson returned a half hour later to announce the winners, he began by thanking the five judges. He joked that eating cookies was a tough job, but he hoped he would be chosen for that brutal task next year! Everyone laughed. Then he thanked all those who had entered the contest. He told us there had been eighteen entries, and the judges used a scoring system to pick their favorite based on taste, texture, presentation, and uniqueness.

He started by announcing that the third-place winner was Darlene Wright, who'd entered her Coconut Surprise cookies. She took to the stage for her ribbon, and everyone clapped. I squeezed Polly's hand. The second-place winner was Mrs. Olson, who'd entered her Marshmallow Delight cookies. I could see the surprise and disappointment on her face that she hadn't won first place. Polly took a deep breath. She either won first place, or she didn't place at all. This was nerve-racking!

The chairperson congratulated both Mrs. Wright and Mrs. Olson. Then he reminded all of us that the first-place winner would walk away with a $5,000 check. Someone came onto the stage then with a check that must have been eight feet long. That didn't do anything to calm Polly's nerves. I squeezed her hand again, this time a little harder, and whispered that everything would be okay.

"With much anticipation," he began, "I believe we're ready to announce the first-place winner. Polly Peterson, please step forward. Your Christmas Kringle cookies have been determined the best cookie winner by our panel of judges! Congratulations! And for those who don't know, Polly owns Polly's Peppermint Shop on Main Street. I bet you'll all be able to taste her Christmas Kringle cookies before long!"

My heart skipped a beat, and Polly and I jumped up and down with joy. With the applause still roaring, Polly accepted a trophy shaped like a cookie and stood by the huge $5,000 check. I noticed then that the memo on the check said The Best Baker in Town. Truly, she was the best baker, and now she had the proof! Several people took her picture as she held the check as best she could. Even the local paper was there to capture the moment. There was no wiping the smile from Polly's face.

She was offered the microphone and thanked the judges for voting for her and thanked her customers who had been supporting her shop in the brief time it had been open. Through tears, she said this award was the nicest recognition she'd ever received, and she was putting the trophy right next to a picture of her grandma, who'd taught her everything she knew about baking.

Once she left the stage, Mrs. Olson was the first to approach her with congratulations. She told Polly that she looked forward to buying a few of her first-place cookies next week.

On the way back to the shop, Polly couldn't thank me enough for pressing her to enter the contest. I reminded her that she did all the hard work, and the whole town was about to benefit from it. With all the publicity from the contest, soon everyone in town would be lining up at Polly's Peppermint Shop.

Aunt Susan greeted us at the door as we arrived at the shop. She'd already heard the news, and so had two dozen other folks who were lined up. Shortly afterward Harry from the hardware store came over and asked if he could prepare a lease for Polly. She nodded and gave Harry a hug for thinking of her. We popped open a bottle of champagne to share in celebration of this good day.

I announced, "Here's to Polly's Peppermint Shop, the new home of the award-winning Christmas Kringle cookies!" Everyone cheered.

Sometimes someone else sees our potential more clearly than we do. Believe them, and believe in yourself.

Polly's Peppermint Cake

3½ cups cake flour, spooned and leveled

2½ tsp baking powder

¾ tsp baking soda

½ tsp kosher salt

1 cup unsalted butter, at room temperature

1½ cups granulated sugar

6 large egg whites, at room temperature

2 tsp pure vanilla extract

1½ cups buttermilk, at room temperature

1 recipe of 7-Minute Frosting (see the following recipe)

3 crushed candy canes (about ¼ cup), divided

Store-bought peppermint bark, chopped for decorating

1. Preheat the oven to 325° F. Lightly line three 8-inch round cake pans with greased parchment paper.

2. In a mixing bowl, whisk together the flour, baking powder, baking soda, and salt. Set aside.

3. In a separate bowl, beat the butter and sugar with an electric mixer on medium-high speed until pale and fluffy, about 3–4 minutes. Add the egg whites one at a time until they're incorporated after each addition. Beat in the vanilla. Reduce the mixer speed to low and beat

in the flour mixture just until incorporated. Divide the batter among the three prepared pans.

4. Bake until a wooden toothpick inserted in the center comes out clean, about 25–30 minutes. Cool the cakes in the pans on wire racks for 5 minutes, and then invert onto racks to cool completely.

5. Place one cake layer on a cake stand or plate. Top with 1 cup frosting and sprinkle with half of the crushed candy canes. Repeat one more time. Cover the top and sides of the cake with the remaining frosting. Press the bark into the frosting on the sides of the cake.

7-Minute Frosting

1 cup sugar

¼ tsp salt

½ tsp cream of tartar

2 egg whites

3 tbsp water

1 tsp peppermint or vanilla extract

1. In a stainless-steel heavy-bottomed saucepan, combine all the ingredients except the vanilla.

2. Heat the mixture on medium-low and beat with an electric hand mixer constantly until the icing is fluffy and stiff peaks form when the beaters are removed, about 7 minutes.

3. Remove the pan from the heat and stir in the extract.

Note: If you like a lot of frosting, you can double this recipe, but you might need to increase the time in Step 2 to 14 minutes.

Christmas in July

My husband John and I have been married for fifteen years, and we have no kids. I work from home as an editor, and he's hoping to become the president of the advertising agency he works for. One of our neighbors in the condo complex is Ivy Broadwater. She's single, thirty-nine, and makes her living as an accountant, working from home.

We have a nice size pool to share at the complex. Ivy never gets in, but she enjoys reading books out there as she sits completely covered beneath an umbrella. I rarely see her speak to anyone but me. She always seems unhappy, but I'm not sure why. I've tried to engage her in conversation to change her mood, but my efforts haven't had an influence so far.

Ivy comes out to the pool around eleven each morning and returns to her place about an hour later. One day I decided to join her.

"Hey, Ivy," I said. "Do you mind if I join you today?"

She shook her head, so I pulled up the lawn chair next to hers.

We exchanged small talk for a minute, and then I asked, "So, do you have family who live near here?"

"No."

"Oh, that's too bad. What do you like to do with your free time when you're not working?"

"I don't have any."

"Free time is hard to come by sometimes, isn't it? I see you sitting out here by the pool every day. Can you swim?"

She just shook her head at my last question. I kept talking to her anyway about what I'd been doing and how I was looking forward to seeing some family next month. She never seemed to get annoyed by our one-sided conversation.

The next day was especially hot, so more children than usual came to enjoy the pool. Judging from Ivy's scowl, kids seemed to annoy her. It was almost humorous to watch.

"Ivy, I brought you some tomatoes. It's been good weather for them. Can you believe the heat we're having this summer? I prefer winter. How about you?" She just nodded.

"Actually, I'm a big fan of Christmas," I continued. "It's such a happy time of year, and I love all the lights. John and I leave the white ones in our kitchen all year long so we can use them as night lights. Do you put up any lights besides those on your tree?"

"No, I don't put up any lights."

"What about on your tree?"

She shook her head. "I don't decorate one."

"Really? No tree? What about other decorations?"

"Trees are messy, and I don't entertain."

"John and I don't entertain much either, but I still decorate. He knows it makes me happy, so he tolerates it. As a child, I always had a wonderful Christmas and believed in Santa Claus till I was quite old. I know it's crazy, but Christmas is the perfect time for giving and for celebrating the birth of Jesus. My family had a manger scene we put in the front yard every year, and it was a big deal for one of us to get to lay baby Jesus in the crib. We also went Christmas caroling with my cousins. I'll never forget what it was like walking through the nursing homes and seeing all the old people. Some of them would be sitting out in the hallway looking dejected until they heard us burst forth in song. They really brightened up. They were so thankful. Have you ever done that?"

"No, my father was in the service, so we traveled a lot. We really didn't celebrate Christmas."

"Oh, I see. So, you didn't celebrate at all?"

"It was just like any other day."

"Do you have siblings?"

She shook her head.

"I have sisters and brothers, and Christmas was a big deal for us. All the activity started right after Thanksgiving. It was fun looking at the catalog to make our list for Santa. Do you have a favorite holiday?"

"Not really. Before I worked from home, I used to volunteer to work on the holidays so others could be with their families. It mattered none to me."

"That was so nice of you, Ivy. You may not have realized it at the time, but you were giving them a special gift."

"Oh, I doubt that. Well, I need to get back inside and get some work done. Thanks again for the tomatoes."

"You're welcome." And with that, she walked away.

That evening when John came home, I started babbling about my conversation with Ivy. He seemed to be only half listening until I told him she'd never had Christmas as a child. He shook his head as I continued to tell her story.

"Well, what did you really expect? She's chosen to be a recluse. The responses she gets from others are all her doing. She obviously likes being left alone, and you should respect that."

"It's just so sad, John. I wish I would have known about this last Christmas so we could have invited her over."

The rest of the night, I kept thinking about what I could do to bring Ivy a moment of joy. It broke my heart when she said she'd never celebrated Christmas. Christmas was five months away, but perhaps there was a way to show Ivy some Christmas spirit now.

I thought perhaps I could give Ivy a Christmas experience she'd never had. If I could just get her inside our place, I'd think of something. John thought I was wasting my time with her, but I decided that I'd ask her if she'd like to come over for lunch.

The next day, like clockwork, Ivy appeared by the pool. When I joined her this time, she actually smiled. I didn't say anything for a bit while I checked my phone for texts and emails. I finally got the nerve to ask her over.

"Ivy, I was wondering if you'd join me for lunch tomorrow. I hate eating lunch alone, and I love to cook. I promise I won't keep you from your work for long. What do you think?"

"Okay, but I can't stay more than an hour. Also, I'm a picky eater, so please don't go to a lot of trouble."

"Oh, sure, I understand. How about noon, when you usually go back inside?"

She nodded and returned to reading. Most folks would have thanked me or maybe even offered to bring something, but Ivy was different. For all I knew, she might not even show up.

As I left her, I told her I looked forward to seeing her. My mind was going crazy with ideas for lunch. Should I expose her to a little Christmas or just go about making her a simple sandwich? Thoughts of a Christmas-themed lunch made me smile. She'll really think I'm nuts, but it'll be fun.

I started making a list of all the Christmassy things I could do or make. I normally only cook Brunswick stew on Christmas Eve, but John would be delighted if I made a pot in the middle of the summer. I'd start it tonight, as it takes a while to prepare. Thankfully, John had a dinner meeting and wouldn't be home until late.

In December, I typically have a tree in every room, but one tree would suffice for this occasion, and I just happened to keep a decorated one in our basement storage room. I carried it up the stairs and put it in the corner of the living room. Voilà! That was easy! I started thinking about Christmas cookies. It wouldn't be a Christmas celebration without them.

While the stew cooked and the cookies baked, I brought up some decorations, including the large wreath that we always hang above our fireplace. The place was starting to smell and look like Christmas. Oh, I wish it really were!

I put a red tablecloth on the table and set out the matching napkins. I remembered the candle and holly centerpiece that we kept in the hall closet and put it out too. Locating the

Christmas music was easy because I played our favorite CD throughout the year, not just in December. Things were starting to look festive!

When I placed the tree skirt around the bottom of our tree, I realized I needed a gift to make it feel like Christmas. Was I pushing things too far by giving Ivy a gift? I had a regift drawer in the bedroom, so I opened it to see what might be suitable. I located a couple of blank journals, but the one that said *My many wishes* on the front would work. I stuffed it into a Christmas gift bag and topped it with some red tissue paper.

When John walked in at eight, his look was priceless.

"You really did it, didn't you? How did you get that tree up here?"

"You know how I am when I set my mind to something, honey."

"Yes, I sure do. Hey, what do I smell cooking?"

"Your favorite Brunswick stew and Aunt Jessi's chocolate cookies. The cookies are still warm, so help yourself."

John was more than happy to give in to my silliness if it meant stew and cookies. He was quiet the rest of the evening.

As I lay wide awake in bed that night, I thought about the Christmas quilts I had tucked away. I got out of bed to set them out so I could show them to Ivy tomorrow. Finally, I was ready to give in to sleep. I prayed my efforts tonight would be worth it.

"I'm glad you didn't ask me to play Santa," John joked the next morning. "Are you going to keep up the decorations if she's a no-show?"

"Well, maybe, but you'll end up being the winner with more cookies and Brunswick stew. I kind of like having Christmas in July, though."

John wished me good luck and left for work. I quickly set the table and put the stew on low heat.

At eleven o'clock, I looked out the window and didn't see Ivy by the pool. I kept busy getting ready. Then twelve o'clock came. Still no Ivy. I'd been stood up and started scolding myself for going to all this trouble.

Around twelve ten, Ivy approached our door. She had on a long-sleeved dress, and her hair was pulled back. I rushed to open the door to greet her.

"Hi, Ivy!" I said with a big smile. "Come on in."

When she stepped inside and saw the tree, she stood speechless. She looked back at the door like she might leave.

"I don't understand," she said, concerned.

"Merry Christmas!" I said cheerfully. "I decided to make our lunch fun and wanted to give you a taste of Christmas."

"You do know it's July, don't you?" She looked puzzled.

I chuckled and nodded. "I do! I thought this might get our minds off the heat. Go ahead and have a seat while I pour us some refreshing cranberry juice. You gave me a reason to cook something special today. I made a traditional Brunswick stew that I cook every Christmas Eve. I had fun doing this for you."

"You really shouldn't have," she said, shaking her head.

She started looking around at the Christmas tree and everything else once she sat down at the table. I began explaining some of the other decorations as I filled our bowls.

"This artificial tree is normally in our bedroom at Christmas, and we put a live tree here in the living room. I keep this tree in the basement, so it was easy to haul upstairs last night."

"You're not going to turn on the fireplace, are you?" she joked. She was starting to feel more relaxed, I think.

I chuckled. "I guess I can skip the fire considering it's 90 degrees! But I did make our favorite Christmas cookie recipe and have a tin of them for you to take home."

"You really didn't have to do all this," she said, sounding a little embarrassed that I'd gone to all the trouble. "So, do you play Christmas music all year, or only when you have Christmas in July?"

I smiled. "I would love to play it all year, but John would kill me if I did. And, for the record, he thought I was nuts doing all this today, but he's thrilled to have the stew and the cookies."

I did most of the talking through the meal. I would have liked a compliment on the stew, but it didn't happen. She did appear to enjoy it, though. When we finished, I suggested that we retire to the living room.

"I have a little gift for you, Ivy," I said as I held out the bag I'd prepared last night. "It's not Christmas without a little present."

It took her a minute to take it from my hand, and she didn't look at me when she did.

"I'm sorry, but I have no gift for you. I'm curious why it matters to you so much that I don't celebrate Christmas."

"I didn't expect you to give me anything today, Ivy. I just wanted you to experience the joy that I feel at Christmastime. The gift is related to all the reading you do. I thought maybe you'd want to use it to reflect on your dreams for the future." I was afraid I'd offended her by pushing Christmas on her like I did.

Ivy finally opened her gift bag and offered a quiet thank-you.

While we were sitting in the living room, she kept running her hand across my mother's Christmas quilt that was lying next to her on the couch.

"Isn't it marvelous to run your hands across all those handmade stitches on the quilt?" I asked. "My mother was an avid quilter, but I never took to it myself. Every time she made a quilt, she said it was for one of her future grandchildren. Well, that's not happening yet anyway. She called this one a Log Cabin quilt. Do you or your mother quilt?"

She looked sad as she answered. "My mother was a quilter, too, and when I saw this pattern, it reminded me of her. Unfortunately, she passed away several years ago, and I have none of her quilts."

"Oh, I'm truly sorry. I'm sure whoever has the quilts now would love for you to have one."

She shook her head. "You don't know Aunt Agnes. She inherited almost everything because she took care of my mom when she got really sick toward the end. I couldn't take off work to care for her because I needed every penny to pay the bills."

"Oh, Ivy. That must hurt."

"I do appreciate all the trouble you went to today. I'm happy you have such good Christmas memories." She glanced at her watch, saying, "Oh my! I didn't realize how late it was. The time has flown by. I'd better get home now." She then rose from the couch.

"Are you sure you have to go?" I asked as she walked toward the door. "It's been so nice to really visit with you instead of our usual short exchange by the pool. Now, don't forget your gift and the cookies. Oh, and I want you to have one more thing."

She looked at me strangely, and I continued. "Ivy, I'd love for you to take this Log Cabin quilt to remember your mother by. I have plenty of quilts, and my mother would want you to have this one."

"Oh, I can't possibly do that," she countered.

"Yes, you can," I assured her. "Christmas is all about making someone happy who doesn't expect it. The thought of you taking care of this quilt makes me smile. Quilts are made to be loved."

Her eyes filled with tears. She accepted the quilt in her arms and squeezed my hand. She finally realized that my goal was to make her happy.

"Thank you," she whispered as she left.

As I watched Ivy leave, I thought about our time together. I wasn't sure what to expect today, but I was pleased with how things went. By the time John came home, I had most of the Christmas decorations put away.

"Well, did she show up?" he asked.

I smiled and nodded. "Yes, she did, and it was the best Christmas in July I've ever had!"

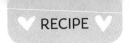
Brunswick Stew

One 5-pound whole chicken, or the equivalent in chicken breasts

4 cups chopped potatoes

4 cups whole canned tomatoes

4 cups small butter beans

4 cups corn

Salt, pepper, paprika, and sugar to taste

1. Place the chicken in a stock pot and cover with approximately 2 quarts of cold water. Cook on high until boiling.

2. Lower the heat and continue to cook until the meat separates from the bones easily, approximately 45 minutes.

3. Remove the chicken from the pot and allow it to cool.

4. Debone the chicken and remove its skin.

5. Chop the chicken into bite-size pieces and return it to its broth.

6. Add the potatoes, tomatoes, beans, and corn.

7. Cook on low, stirring often to prevent sticking.

8. Remove from the heat when the potatoes are tender when pierced with a fork, about 1 hour.

9. Season with salt, pepper, and paprika. You can also add a little sugar if you'd like.

The Empty Christmas Stocking

When I was younger, we always spent Christmas at my grandmother's house. One thing I vividly remember was seeing Christmas stockings hung on her fireplace mantle. Santa always left two of them empty.

My mother explained that those two stockings belonged to family members who were no longer with us. My grandpa was one of them, and then a cousin, Carolyn, who died in a car accident. I was too young to question the idea of the empty Christmas stocking, so I just accepted it.

When my grandmother died and my sister was born, we spent Christmas at our own house. It didn't take me long to notice that my mother was carrying on the tradition her mother had. There was an empty stocking for my grandpa and grandma. How did Santa know they were no longer with us?

Years went by, and when I got married, I assured my husband we would have no empty stockings hanging above our small fireplace.

Two years later, I became pregnant and was told it was going to be a boy. We were elated and picked out the name John David before he was born. We wanted to name him after my husband and his father. I had a stocking custom-made to match the ones my husband and I used.

I was overwhelmed when John David III was born, making me doubtful about having more children. I felt like I hadn't slept in months, which sometimes made me cranky, and our house was a wreck.

When our little boy was eighteen months old, we had the shock of a lifetime. He fell on the sidewalk and hit his head pretty hard. Through the testing the hospital did, we learned he had a sizable brain tumor that required an operation and chemo treatments at the children's hospital. It was like living a nightmare.

Days before John David would have turned two, he passed away in my arms. We knew our lives would never be the same. We were devastated that our only son didn't have the chance to grow up. After a lot of discussion, we made the difficult decision not to have more children.

Four months after his death, the Christmas holidays were approaching. I dreaded Christmas that year, knowing our little boy wouldn't be with us. I didn't want to decorate at all, but my husband said that would magnify our grief. With his encouragement, I brought up the boxes of Christmas decorations from the basement and stacked them in the living room. The first box I opened contained our Christmas stockings, and John David's was right on top. I burst into tears and walked away. I wasn't ready for this.

The next week, I needed to pick up some supplies at Target. Christmas decorations filled the store. I stopped in my tracks when I saw a small, red fire truck ornament hanging in the toy aisle. I thought of John David and knew he would have absolutely loved it. Every time he saw or heard a fire truck, he got so excited that we would stop whatever we were doing to listen to or watch it. I couldn't resist buying the perfect ornament for our son to place in his stocking.

Later that night, I told my husband about the experience and showed him the ornament. He saw the desperation on my face and agreed that it needed to go in John David's stocking.

On Christmas Eve, we hung the three stockings and placed the fire truck in our son's. As we stood back to admire them, we hung onto each other in sadness. Were we just setting ourselves up for more grief and disappointment? I thought of my grandmother's tradition and began to understand why she hung the empty stockings.

John David wouldn't be able to look inside his stocking, but he would forever be in our hearts. He would still be spending Christmas with us each year. We hadn't forgotten him.

TEN CHRISTMAS GIFTS
FOR YOURSELF

1. *Forgive yourself for not getting all the things done that you wanted to before Christmas.*

2. *Start reading the book that you've put off.*

3. *Find your roots. There's lots of free help out there.*

4. *Forgive the person who has wronged you. Set yourself free.*

5. *Take a leap with a hairstyle change.*

6. *Attend a Christmas Eve service and listen to the Christmas story.*

7. *In total darkness, admire the silence and glow of Christmas lights.*

8. *Build a snowman or make a snow angel.*

9. *Cook a meal of only your favorite foods.*

10. *Give time instead of money to your favorite charity. It's the best gift of all!*

Welcome to Christmas Town!

In Christmas Town, the cheeks are rosy, the rooftops are snowy, and all the children are well behaved.

Who wouldn't want to live in Christmas Town? If you love Christmas as much as I do, you'd move there tomorrow.

The mayor of the town, of course, is Santa Claus. His council are the elves who work together for the love of Christmas.

Candy canes line the sidewalks, and those walking their paths know they're going somewhere wonderful. Sleds and large sleighs are the preferred methods of transportation. The houses and stores are made of gingerbread.

Churches are the source of most of the Christmas music you can hear day and night. They have manger scenes out front to remind us of the true meaning of Christmas. Carolers make their way around town, singing to their hearts' content. Those who witness the caroling pass out hot chocolate and marshmallows when the singers arrive at the door.

Nights are wintery and cold, so logs crackle in the fireplaces.

Christmas delicacies are aplenty. There's a bakery on every corner in town, emitting aromas of cinnamon, sugar cookies, Christmas pudding, fruitcake, and every kind of homemade bread. Outside the shops, someone is roasting chestnuts on an open fire.

Household kitchens keep their Christmas menu traditions of roast turkey, duck, and homemade stuffing. It's cranberry season, so cranberry relish and other dishes using the tart berry abound.

At the center of every household and business are live Christmas trees. Fragrances of cedar, pine, and spruce offer fond memories of years past. Each family decorates their tree using unique ornaments, most of which are handmade. A traditional shining star is placed atop the tree representing the Star of Bethlehem. Candles are lit on the feather trees only on Christmas Eve, and candles glow from every windowsill. The tree is also the gathering point for the family when they sing or open gifts. Some families decide not to wrap the gifts and just present them under the tree.

The stockings hang on the fireplace mantle for Mayor Santa to fill. The sweet treats are the kids' reward for being good all year long.

Christmas Town is like no other. The smells and sounds are a delight each day, but only a Christmas wish can take you there. You must leave all your troubles and sadness behind so Christmas Town can welcome you with its special spirit.

A WRITER'S CHRISTMAS

A writer's vision of Christmas may just be snow

Or it may be Christmas trees all aglow.

Maybe it's a picture of cookies and pie

Or lots of presents with bows to tie.

Finding the words to describe Santa Claus

Is like choosing the charity with the best cause.

We could list the carols everyone sings

Or describe the romance that Christmas brings.

Writing about Christmas is a joy at best.

There's the Christmas story, and you know the rest.

The important message explains the season.

The birth of Jesus is the real reason.

Merry Christmas!

A Santa for Everyone

Bart Holiday has been a neighbor of ours for as long as my husband and I have lived in this neighborhood. We do our best to watch out for him, and other neighbors do the same. He's been living alone as a widower for a number of years. Despite that, he's the jolliest person we know.

Cooking is a favorite pastime of Bart's, and his big, round belly is proof of how much he enjoys food. He also maintains a full, white, fluffy beard, which makes him the perfect Santa Claus every Christmas. Some of his friends even call him Santa year-round.

Like my husband and me, Bart and his wife never had any children. Maybe that's why he loves children so much and lights up playing Santa. He wears his red suit and Santa hat almost daily from just after Thanksgiving until Christmas morning.

One day in early December, I brought Bart his favorite chicken casserole. He calls it Comfort Casserole because during his busy season of playing Santa, he doesn't have time to cook, and the dish brings him love and comfort on frigid days.

I usually just drop off the casserole, but this time I stayed and visited with him. As he poured me a cup of coffee from his 1980s percolator, I asked if he felt up to playing Santa again.

"Oh, sure," he said, patting his belly. "It's my excuse for keeping this big tummy! At the age of 77, I know I have to keep moving and doing what I can. And when I see the joy I bring each year to the kiddos, the time and effort I put in are always worth it."

"I admire what you do, Bart. Do you have a busy schedule coming up?"

He didn't check his calendar or his phone to give me his answer. "I always do. One place I'll visit will be the Fulbright Nursing Home. I'm never sure how long that will take because I know so many of the folks there, and we have fun visiting."

He paused and smiled before continuing. "Oh, and Manning's department store wants me there for an entire afternoon. And I'm sure you know Elsie Collins down the street. She wants me to stop by and visit her grandchildren. Those are a few of the lineups I have, but there are a few dozen more."

"Wow! That's a big commitment on your part!" I said, shaking my head. "Is it always like that?"

"Some days I have a lighter schedule, depending on how I feel." He rubbed his left kneecap, saying, "My knees have been talking to me lately, so I have to pace myself. As I think about it, Mary, maybe you would like to come with me tomorrow when I make some of my rounds. I could use a little help passing out those socks and all."

"Socks? Not candy?" I asked.

"Yeah," he said, chuckling proudly. "I have candy canes, too, but they're most excited about their socks from Santa."

"Why socks?"

"Because you can't get to sleep if your feet are cold. Those folks need more warmth than sugar."

"I see. So, your bag here is full of socks?"

He nodded. "It sure is. A sack of socks!"

"Then I'd love nothing more than to join you, Bart," I answered. "You probably know I'm a freelance writer. I could compose a story for the *Gazette* newspaper about this experience if you'll allow me to."

We agreed to meet up early the next morning. I planned to bring along my yellow notepad for writing notes. My phone would suffice for any photos I wanted to take.

At eight o'clock, Bart pulled up in his red pickup truck. It was good timing, as I'd just finished my breakfast.

"So, where are we off to first this morning?" I asked, shivering from the cold.

"The folks at the Fulbright Nursing Home are eating their breakfast now, so I thought we could pop in and surprise them."

"Socks for everyone, right?"

"Yes, ma'am. They won't let me give out candy canes there."

I took a deep breath as we walked in the door of the nursing home. It didn't take long for Bart to yell out "Ho, Ho, Ho" as we entered the dining hall.

Gasps of delight and laughter erupted when the residents saw Bart. Some were able to get out of their chairs, but most couldn't. He approached the ladies and asked if they'd been good the past year. Their embarrassed red faces in response were priceless. When he'd go up to the men to ask if they'd been good, he often heard, "No! That's no fun!"

I bet the residents wondered what I was doing there. Donning a Santa hat, I just smiled and occasionally said, "Merry Christmas."

The two of us went from table to table. It was my job to make sure Bart didn't overlook anyone with the gift of socks. I saw a few residents tear up when they were given their socks. This visit from Santa made them feel young again.

The staff wanted socks and hugs from Santa also, so they followed us out to the hallway. Then Bart went to specific rooms to visit a few people who were confined to their beds. One lady turned her head like the Almighty had come into her room. Bart quickly acknowledged her and even gave her a kiss on the cheek, which caused quite a stir. I had goose bumps just watching the exchange. The woman clutched her new socks against her chest as if they were the only gift she might receive.

As Bart made his way down the hall to leave, he shouted, "Merry Christmas, and Happy New Year to all!" I knew for many this would be the highlight of their Christmas. I had no words for what Santa had accomplished on this visit.

The next stop was at a building I was unfamiliar with. Bart said it was called the Hampton House. I looked at him for an explanation.

"This will be a hard place to visit, Mary," he warned as he pulled into a parking spot. "You're going to see a lot of kids who don't have a home for Christmas. Hampton House is basically an orphanage for children under twelve. These kids are true Santa believers, trust me. Their wishes are well beyond what Santa can bring." He shook his head in sadness.

"Well, let's see if we can bring them some cheer," I said.

We met the administrator as soon as we entered. She knew we'd be coming and alerted us that the kids were having their lunch.

The joy of seeing Santa lit up faces everywhere. Some left the table and ran up to him for a hug. Others were in high chairs, and I wondered how on earth they got here. I was determined to make sure Bart gave everyone a pair of socks, but the kids vocalized some other gifts they wanted for Christmas. They began shouting over one another to get his attention. Some cried because they weren't able to get out of their chairs. The staff looked distressed because they wanted the kids to finish their lunch.

One little girl about four years old tugged on my jacket and asked if her mommy was coming to get her for Christmas. I took a deep breath.

"I bet she's going to try," I managed to say. That's all it took for her to smile. Thank goodness we were ushered out the door soon after that because I was about to burst into tears.

"Bart," I began, "you gave so much joy to those children today. How often do you come here?"

He shook his head sadly. "They only let me come once during the holidays. They have another Santa who comes on Christmas Eve."

We then headed downtown to an area I normally tried to avoid.

"Bart, this neighborhood isn't very safe to drive through," I warned.

"That's why we're here," he informed me. "See those tents among the trees and those along the road over there?" I nodded.

"Well, I know a couple of those folks personally," he continued. "Homelessness is a real concern. I want you to stay in the truck for our last stop, Mary. Some of these folks are on drugs, and you never know what their reaction will be when they see a pretty woman like you. They all know me as the Santa who brings them warm socks at Christmas."

"Oh, Bart, you're really something!" I said as he shut the door of the truck.

I rolled down the window and stayed inside the vehicle as Santa advised. He bellowed his loud "Ho, Ho, Ho" to get their attention, but some were pretty zonked out, wrapped in blankets. A few dozen came out of their tents and were happy to get their pair of socks. One man had no shoes on despite the deathly cold temperatures. A young woman looked to be about seven months pregnant and was happy to receive the socks. Santa also gave these folks candy canes. Some wanted to hug Santa, but he kept moving. It was so hard to see these neighbors up close. They had so little.

They didn't want Bart to leave, and that made me nervous. Some were yelling things I didn't understand. I bet they wondered who the lady was in Santa's truck.

On our way home, I tried to think of the right words to thank Bart for the good he'd done and the perspective he'd shown me. His acts were priceless and memorable.

Bart was modest when I tried to praise him. He brushed it off like his actions were no big deal, but I knew it was for all those he'd visited today. He told me he'd be making more stops tomorrow. He wanted to give those who needed it most an ounce of hope and joy, not to mention warm feet for the winter.

"Thanks so much for letting me come along with you, Bart. You really opened my eyes today."

"I don't know how much longer I can keep doing this, but I'll do it as long as I can. I do know that I'm looking forward to your Comfort Casserole to warm my belly tonight. I thank you so very much for thinking of me."

"You're welcome," I responded, and I gave him a hug. "I'll write my article and show it to you before I send it in."

"That's not necessary, Mary. I could tell you were touched and that your heart is in the right place. I appreciated having your company today."

Snowflakes were beginning to fall as I came in the door to the house. I prepared some hot chocolate and put on a pair of heavy socks similar to the ones Bart had given away to so many today. I reflected on what a kind gift those socks were and on his wise words about not being able to go to sleep when your feet are cold. He provided so many with warm feet and warm hearts today.

There was so much I could write about today's experience. I was mostly a bystander witnessing the love of one man for people he didn't even know. He made a difference today, and he inspired me to find a path of my own to bring others some of that cheer and comfort.

Comfort Casserole

Two 10-ounce packages frozen broccoli

2 cups diced cooked chicken

2 cans condensed cream of chicken soup

1 cup salad dressing or mayonnaise

1 tsp lemon juice

½ tsp curry powder

½ cup shredded sharp cheddar cheese

1 cup soft bread crumbs

1 tbsp butter

1. Preheat the oven to 350° F. Grease an 8 × 11-inch baking dish.

2. Bring a pot of salted water to a boil over high heat. Place the broccoli in the pot, and cook until tender.

3. Arrange the broccoli in the baking dish, and layer the chicken on top.

4. In a bowl, combine the soup, salad dressing, lemon juice, and curry powder. Pour over the chicken and sprinkle with cheese.

5. In a bowl, combine the bread crumbs with the butter and sprinkle on top of the casserole.

6. Bake until golden brown, about 25–30 minutes.

The Chosen One

The Ever Holly Christmas Tree Farm in Oregon grows thousands of Christmas trees every year. Oregon sells more trees than any other state; it surpasses its closest rival, North Carolina, by almost two million trees.

Located on this massive Christmas tree farm are many trees hoping to achieve seven-year growth, which is believed to be the timeline for the perfect Christmas tree.

Just like humans, some trees respond well to maintenance and become healthy, whereas others succumb to disease. Fraser fir and Douglas fir are the most popular fir varieties for Christmas. People also seem to like simple pine trees. On my last visit to the Christmas tree farm, I noticed a particular pine tree struggling. It was small and couldn't seem to catch up with its neighboring pines, no matter how hard it tried.

As a frequent visitor to the farm, I started paying attention to the little tree I named Tiny Piney. It started growing along with the others, but soon this tree was overshadowed by its neighboring trees. As the hard snowstorms fell, it was often hard to find Tiny Piney.

As the Christmas season neared, families came in to select their favorite tree. Wholesale buyers, too, came in to cut trees. Various trees were carted away, but never Tiny Piney.

As the storms worsened, Tiny Piney began losing limbs, making it even less desirable. The less-than-mighty pine shook its limbs to draw attention to itself, but the tactic never worked. No one wanted this small tree.

It was the last weekend before Christmas when I approached Tiny Piney up close. I dusted off the snow so I could better determine its shape. Many of its side branches drooped, but the top branch for a star stood perfectly straight. Tiny Piney was saying, "Take me! I'm perfect!"

I smiled and told the employee I wanted to take home this particular tree. He questioned my choice and even showed me other trees in better shape.

But I insisted on taking Tiny Piney. This tree no one else wanted reminded me of the unkempt rescue dog named Patches I used to have. I knew Patches was the one for me, just like I knew this tree was.

Tiny Piney found a place in my home where I normally placed a smaller tree. Its smell was powerful, despite its appearance. When I placed the shining star on its top branch, I knew Tiny Piney felt proud.

All it took was for someone to see in this tree what others couldn't. Is there a Tiny Piney in your life waiting to be chosen?

Why Can't Christmas Just Be Over?

You may have heard that you can't be lonely in a crowd, but that's simply not true. I've lived long enough to hear others' echoes of loneliness. When you're lonely in a crowd, it feels like no one sees you. They may see your body, but they don't see your thoughts and your mind.

Carolyn had been lonely in her marriage for more than twenty years. She had a handsome, successful husband and all the luxuries that came with that. She thought life would get better when their first child was born, but instead it seemed to make matters worse. Their near-perfect daughter became the love of her husband's life but didn't do much to bond the marital union.

Carolyn hoped the gaiety and beautiful decor of Christmas would lift her mood, but she felt disengaged. Why couldn't Christmas just be over?

Helen had been in assisted living for a year. Her children lived out of state, and most of her friends were deceased. At eighty, she didn't feel like making new friends, and hearing from her ailing friends only made her feel worse. When

Christmas came, it reminded her of all the beautiful years she no longer had, and it made her sad. She used to decorate her home lavishly this time of year, but now that she was in assisted living, she had just the simplest wreath on her door. She felt small and unimportant.

Staff bragged about their personal lives and how they were spending Christmas. They couldn't wait for their time off away from the residents. Carolers sang in the lobby, and there was even a goofy Santa Claus one day, but they treated the residents like sad children, and it only made Helen feel worse. It was hard to pretend to enjoy the festivities when she was crying inside. Why couldn't this Christmas just be over?

Jinni was about to be fourteen and had no siblings. Her mother was loving, but her father never let her forget that he always wanted a son. She tried to appease him by playing several sports, but he didn't appreciate her efforts, and he criticized her performance. There were times that Jinni felt like the third wheel when she was around her parents. The strain affected her relationships with her girlfriends and made her feel unworthy of love.

They always spent Christmas with her mother's big family, which meant being around her cousins. It seemed her cousins had plenty to brag about. They certainly seemed happier than she was. She was a good listener, but no one asked about her life. Did anyone even see her? Why couldn't her Christmas just be over?

Richard became a widower at the young age of sixty. After being married to the same woman all his life, he had no desire to replace what he'd had with her. He'd just retired from the plastics company he'd been employed by for most of his career. Everyone cheered him on at his retirement party, telling him how happy he'd be to finally travel and do all the hunting and fishing he wanted. It all sounded good to him, but he had no one to enjoy these adventures with. His closest friends still had wives to share their lives with. As time went on, he agreed to be set up with other women, but they only reminded him of the loss of his great love. Besides, he didn't like dating in this new world.

Christmas in his retirement meant there would be no annual holiday party with his coworkers that he so much enjoyed. He'd have to make his own Christmas cheer and spend Christmas Eve with his only son. He didn't put up a tree at his own house, so he agreed to go to his son and daughter-in-law's apartment. They had no children to liven up the holiday, and he was having a hard time feeling joyful. He just wasn't feeling the Christmas spirit.

On Christmas morning, he attended church as he always had, but something was missing. It felt like just yesterday he'd been in church with his wife. But this year it was fast food and TV. Hopefully, there would be a good football game he could watch later to distract him. Why couldn't Christmas just be over?

There's no question that the Christmas season can feel overwhelming for those who feel alone and isolated. Human nature tends to draw us toward happy and positive people rather than those who stand back and watch life go by. Take notice of the latter. They're important.

If you have an opportunity to make someone feel special at Christmas, do it. It's a real gift for them and for you. Christmas should be for everyone. Make those special phone calls, write personal Christmas cards to your loved ones, or better yet, invite others to your home to share your joy. We sometimes assume that everyone has family and friends, but that isn't always the case. Imagine what a difference we could make for them on the holiday and into the new year. Before you know it, they could be saying, "Why can't Christmas be all year long?"

CHRISTMAS ACTS OF KINDNESS

Visit those who are lonely.

Bake bread for those you love.

Make a personalized gift for someone.

Choose your favorite charity, and be generous.

Invite someone to a Christmas service.

Join others in Christmas caroling.

Help someone in need decorate their tree.

Call someone you haven't talked to in a while.

Enclose a personal note in your Christmas cards.

Instead of purchasing a gift for someone,
help them with a chore or a problem.

Put an unexpected Christmas wreath on someone's door.

Consider a personal, handwritten thank-you note
for acts of kindness others have shown you.

A Repurposed Christmas

Repurposing means using an item for a different purpose than it was originally intended. Perhaps you remodeled your bathroom and tore out the old claw-foot tub. You hate to just get rid of it because it's an antique, so you move it to your outside garden and fill it with dirt and colorful flowers.

When my Patchwork Pal Quilt Club met this fall, we began making plans for our Christmas party. Once we settled on a time and place, I suggested we bring a repurposed Christmas gift. Everyone seemed excited by the idea, as they were a creative bunch.

Each wrapped gift would be assigned a number, and we'd draw numbers to determine which gift we'd take home. Some quilters dropped hints on what they might make.

As the Christmas party drew near, excitement was building. Because I was a collector of red-and-white handkerchiefs, I decided my gift would be repurposing them into a dainty apron. After drawing a quick sketch, I decided to cut one handkerchief in half and sew the triangle onto each side of the center handkerchief. The designs of the handkerchiefs were similar, so they complemented each other. I used a red ribbon across the top and for the apron strings. The apron was a vintage style I'd seen elsewhere. I was pleased with the way it turned out, and I hoped the recipient would be as well.

Margaret was hosting the party in her lovely, historic home that was filled with antiques and beautiful china and crystal. Each place setting used a different china pattern and silverware. She varied the cloth napkins to match the color of china used. It made for great conversation. Some of the china she'd inherited, and others she'd found at estate sales and thrift stores.

Her buffet had a large, crystal, champagne punch bowl filled to the brim with punch and topped with an iced Christmas wreath to keep it cool and make it festive. All of us brought a plate of our homemade Christmas cookies for refreshments. Margaret used many of her antique Christmas ornaments as decorations, and in the corner of the dining room was a small antique feather tree that was more than one hundred years old. It always fascinated me to see the green dyed goose feathers wrapped around the wires to resemble pine limbs. Her tree was 4 feet tall and quite worn. It certainly had stories to tell.

George, Margaret's husband, greeted everyone at the door in his old Santa Claus suit he'd worn for many years. The mood was jolly, just as Santa had ordered.

When it came time to open gifts, the loud chatter among the group turned into oohs and aahs. Ellen's gift was the first to be opened. She'd made a Christmas stocking out of a worn red-and-green antique quilt. She used antique lace and pearl buttons to embellish it.

Kelly collected old neckties and made a striking Dresden plate pillow that had black velvet on the back and strips of patterned red-and-green ties sewn in the shape of a wreath on the front. She said she could tell a story about each tie she used.

Maxine created the most unique gift of all: a teddy bear made from her grandmother's old fur coat. It looked so real and like she'd had it professionally done. We all marveled at how in the world she managed to sew with fur. Everyone gave the bear a hug as we passed it around the room.

Betty took a vintage chenille bedspread and made a bed jacket out of it. She told us she'd also made one to give to her grandmother in the hospital. Some didn't know what a bed jacket was, so Betty offered her own personal memories of them.

Louise has had an affinity for buttons since she was ten. She even collects them for button displays to enter in shows. For her gift, she crocheted a button necklace using antique pearl buttons. It was gorgeous. She then surprised all of us with a small button pin she'd made.

Angela is a scrapbooker as well as a quilter, teaching scrapbooking at a hobby shop twice a week. She took an old cookbook and pasted her family recipes into it. When we passed her book around, I jotted down her grandmother's recipe for springerles.

Rosemary repurposed an old, worn, crochet tablecloth to make individual Christmas ornaments and a star for the treetop. She starched them stiff and attached cute ribbon hangers. She, like Louise, had made something for each of us. I couldn't wait to hang my small snowflake from her on our tree. It must have taken her a long time to make all of them.

Laura's gift was next. She'd taken a worn crazy quilt and made a tree skirt out of the best parts. Many of the pieces had names and dates. She used black cotton backing and tied the circle closed with a black ribbon. She told us that the quilt had been in poor repair, which was why she could justify cutting it up. Betty cried when she opened Laura's gift of the tree skirt. She told us her old tree skirt had been destroyed in a fire a couple years ago, so she really appreciated this homemade one.

We were all so impressed with these creative gifts that we decided to do an exchange like this again next year. Everything old can be new again, and sometimes even better than it was before.

What can you repurpose for Christmas this year?

RED AND GREEN

Red is that passionate color in romance and love

But beware of fire, danger, and stop signs above.

Green, red's best contrast, represents life in holly and trees

But its beverage choices are rare unless you're drinking green tea.

When these two colors are beautifully combined,

You can bet it's Merry Christmas time!

Granny's Christmas Wedding

My Granny loved telling me and her grandchildren about her unique wedding to Grandpa. She lived in the country on a farm and was hoping to marry my grandpa, who was considered to be a city boy in his town of eight thousand people.

She described how her parents were skeptical about Grandpa's intentions, but she was determined to marry him, no matter what. Finally, on her birthday that fall, the two got engaged, and Granny began planning their big day.

Granny dreamed of a Christmas wedding in the worst way, but her parents warned her that would be risky with the unpredictability of the winter weather. She didn't need or want a big wedding, but she wanted the church to look festive, as it always did at Christmas. Her church would always have the biggest and most beautiful tree it could find. She bragged about all the antique ornaments from generations back. She told us how much she admired them during services.

Her parents gave in to her dreams of a Christmas wedding, so Granny began planning for a wedding on Christmas

Eve. Her parents told her not to expect much because they just didn't have the money for anything lavish.

The plan was for Granny's sister Norma to be the only bridesmaid, and Grandpa's brother Harold would be the best man. She insisted that Norma wear a bright red dress for the occasion since the wedding would take place the weekend before Christmas. They were lucky to find a red satin one in the Sears Roebuck catalog. Norma was shocked at the high price but went ahead and purchased the dress for her sister's wedding. Harold planned to wear the same suit that he sported for church every Sunday. Norma and Granny would carry green holly bouquets with red berries, and the men would have boutonnieres of holly tied with red bows.

Norma told Granny that her gift to them would be their wedding cake. The bakery was a good distance away, so Granny worried about the cake making it to the church basement. Grandpa's Uncle Charlie promised to make enough homemade ice cream for everyone. Granny said her mother thought it odd to have ice cream for a winter wedding.

Granny told us about trying on her mother's wedding dress. It needed some alterations and some of the lace replaced, but her mother took care of that. Of course, Granny would have preferred a new dress of her own, but that was too much to ask. Granny didn't want to make any waves that could get in the way of her Christmas wedding. Granny's mom remade the veil and attached it to a hair wreath of holly.

Granny had been worried that Grandpa would change his mind about getting married. He was concerned about how they'd survive financially after they were husband and wife. They'd have to move in with his parents till they could afford a little place of their own. Granny said she didn't mind; she just wanted to be married.

Granny said her mom and dad wanted the reception to be in the church basement, but Grandpa's mom and dad thought the shabby basement was too primitive for such an occasion. Granny's parents won the argument. The church basement would be advantageous since it was close to the ceremony, and they were told it would have a fresh coat of paint before the wedding.

The week before the big event, the church basement was painted, but not entirely because the painters ran out of paint and didn't purchase more. Also, Granny wanted red crepe paper to decorate with but was unable to find any. Grandpa kept warning Granny that the forecast for their wedding date was looking grim, but Granny refused to listen.

Mabel would be the church organist. Granny told her to play Christmas music till it was time for her to start walking down the aisle. Mabel wasn't available for a wedding rehearsal, so they didn't have one. Granny didn't let that deter her. All she cared about was saying "I do" to Grandpa.

Granny said Grandpa ignored her the few days before the wedding. He was feeling stressed, and even Granny started having second thoughts about delaying the wedding. Granny said Norma's encouragement kept her going and convinced her that everything would be fine.

Their wedding day was cloudy with a prediction for snow, and the forecast was all everyone could talk about. Granny's mom was ready to say, "I told you so" about having a wedding this time of year. But Granny knew if they could just get through the wedding vows, nothing else mattered.

When Granny finally put on her wedding dress, her face lit up, and nothing could spoil her happiness. Then when she put on her veil, her mother burst into tears of joy. This wedding was going to happen, regardless of the weather.

Snow began falling as soon as Granny crawled in the back seat of her dad's old car. Her mom fussed over her to keep her own nerves down. She started mentally preparing Granny for a low turnout because of the weather.

When Granny walked into the church, she noticed the giant Christmas tree waiting for her. It was the prettiest one yet. She smiled and then accompanied Norma to the side room, waiting for Mabel to play the wedding march.

Granny kept peeking out of the curtain to see who had arrived. So far, the church looked empty. Norma, who looked radiant in her red satin dress, consoled her, saying that folks were just running late because of the weather.

Okay, but where was Grandpa? Granny was getting nervous since she didn't see him. The pastor, who lived next door, had arrived, but there was no sight of the bridegroom.

Mabel began playing the Christmas music as if everything were fine. Granny reminded me that there were no phones to relay messages back then.

Granny tried not to notice that it was now ten minutes past the wedding's start time. Was she being stood up on the biggest day of her life? Finally, Grandpa arrived with his parents. At the time, Granny felt that her parents would have been happy with a no-show from him.

When Grandpa took his place at the altar with Harold and Norma, "Here Comes the Bride" started playing. Just then the church lost power and went completely dark. The men fumbled around trying to do what they could in complete darkness, and the women cried out in distress.

Granny said she screamed and started crying. With all that had happened, she felt the wedding wasn't meant to be, and she just wanted to get away. She ran to the dressing room and grabbed her coat. She headed toward her dad's car, but to his credit, he told her to stay there and talk things over with her groom.

Even in the darkness, Grandpa saw Granny's distress and came running to her. In tears, she informed him that the wedding was off and she wanted him to take her home. The snow was coming down heavier by this point, so without a word, they quickly got into Grandpa's car. She saw folks scatter toward their vehicles. Everyone just wanted to get home.

The car struggled to start, but soon Granny and Grandpa were on their way, driving slowly down the country road. They'd only gone a mile or two when they slid into a ditch in front of a farm. They didn't know whether they should laugh or cry. Grandpa saw that Granny was shivering and convinced her they needed to dash for shelter in the nearby barn or they'd freeze to death in the car before help could come. At this point she didn't care what happened, so she followed his advice.

Granny grabbed a blanket from the back seat to put over her head. She hung on to Grandpa's hand as he led her blindly across the pasture into the red barn. Her best shoes were now muddy as they crossed a ditch. The barn seemed far away, but eventually they reached the door and pulled it open.

The barn was warm and gave them instant shelter from the snow and wind. They spotted hay bales that looked like a good place to rest and regroup, but soon they realized they weren't alone. Two horses were in their stalls and let out snorts. Granny and Grandpa both laughed in surprise. Then they heard another sound coming from above.

"Say there! Who's here?" a gruff man's voice called out.

Grandpa answered, explaining that their car had gotten stuck in a ditch and they needed to take shelter. The elderly man climbed down the ladder and looked them over. He saw Granny's distress and tears and seemed to soften. That's when Grandpa explained that today was supposed to be their wedding day, but the electricity had gone out just as the wedding march was playing.

The farmer stared at them in disbelief and asked them if they still wanted to be married. The two of them looked at each other with affection and nodded yes. It was then that the farmer shared something they weren't expecting.

"If you'd like, I can marry the two of you," he stated. "I happen to be the pastor of the Baptist church down yonder, and I'd be happy to help you wed. Maisie and Silver here in their stalls can be witnesses until we get up to the house where my wife, Ellie, can sign as a witness. Granny and Grandpa then looked at the two horses that appeared to be waiting for their answers.

"Ellie will be happy to make us some hot coffee. You know it's Christmas Eve, don't ya? What do you say?" Grandpa gently turned to Granny for a response.

Granny blushed and agreed to proceed. This certainly wasn't the way she'd envisioned their wedding day, but all that mattered to her was marrying my grandpa.

The farmer asked them to stand next to Silver and Maisie. Then he put on a hat and started reciting the words of matrimony. Following that, he asked them if they still loved one another. When they said yes, he pronounced them husband and wife. It was that simple.

"Now you're free to kiss your bride," he encouraged Grandpa.

They hugged each other tight after they kissed. Neither one of them wanted to let go of the other in the cold barn. Even though the farmer had congratulated Granny and Grandpa, they couldn't believe they were married. It didn't matter what else happened that day. They were married and happy.

Every time Granny told this story, people's first question was always, "You got married in a barn?" I never tired of hearing Granny share the details of that day. Her eyes always twinkled and teared up as she relived those moments.

Granny's story is a good reminder to all about what's important. It's not the fancy decorations and wedding cake but what you make of a challenging situation. Their wedding day was certainly a memorable one, and their marriage every day since has been an example of love, perseverance, and dedication. Granny and Grandpa had their beginnings in a stable, just as the Christ child did.

A Place Called Happy's

I'd never thought too much about the corner bar in our neighborhood called Happy's. I assumed it was for old men, alcoholics, and people looking for company and cheap beer. I did hear someone comment on what great chili they had. My boyfriend, Tim, and I talked often about stopping in there for lunch, but we never did.

My good friend Bea helped out bartending there for some extra cash, and she loved it. She said sometimes it was her only social life.

Bea was over at our apartment one night watching a movie when she boldly asked if we would help out at Happy's on Christmas. She said that the bar was shorthanded for Christmas Day, and they could really use a couple more people. She told us that on Christmas, they always served free chili, which was a big attraction. Their regulars came in, but so did a lot of others.

Tim and I looked at each other, wondering whether she was kidding. Who would want to spend their Christmas in a dark, smoky bar that smelled like beer? My family was out of town, and we had plans to go to Tim's mom's on Christmas Eve. We were planning to just relax at home on Christmas.

"Well, if you put me in the kitchen near the chili, I'll help," Tim answered.

"Thanks, Tim!" Bea cheered.

"You really want to do this, Tim?" I questioned. When he nodded, I said, "Well, if you're in, so am I! It's Christmas!"

"Great, guys!" Bea said. "I promise I'll have you doing simple things like filling water glasses."

"No washing dishes!" I teased.

"I promise," Bea agreed, nodding. "Now, we open at seven in the morning, just so you know."

"Oh my. On Christmas?" I asked.

"They open every day at seven," she replied. "There's a second shift of guys who come in from working the night shift, and they're always hungry. And the retired guys arrive early because they can't sleep and want to get out of the house; they just want that first cup of hot coffee. Daisy, who helps in the kitchen, makes a big batch of hot cinnamon rolls each day. You can smell them as soon as you come in the door. I'm sure she'll be making pans and pans of those for Christmas morning.

"Now I know where to go when I want a cinnamon roll!" Tim answered.

"What you have to understand is that Happy's is home for many of these folks," Bea explained. "It's their family. The regulars come in and take their same seat every day. No one else had better be sitting there, or they'll stare them down." We laughed.

"So, how long will we need to be there?" I asked.

"It's hard telling, but we'll take your help as long as you're willing to give it," Bea said. "We'll be busy till we close, I guarantee you!"

"It sounds like a pretty good business," Tim observed.

"What's kind of a secret about the place is that we get a lot of churchgoers. Folks from the church across the street come in after their meetings. Even the clergy stop in on occasion. Who doesn't enjoy a good hamburger and a cold beer once in a while? I'm sure they'll take advantage of the free chili also. Sometimes we're so busy on Christmas that there's a line outside to get in. The fire marshal will be watching, I'm sure."

"I saw an entire family go in there one day," I reported. "Kids are allowed?"

"Yes, there's a family-friendly dining area. We don't have kids come in often, but everyone makes over them when they're there," Bea said, smiling.

"Well, I'm excited about helping," Tim answered. "I want to learn how to make good chili."

"Good luck with that," Bea noted. "Happy, the owner, brags about his secret recipe, so you might not find out much. But I promise you this will be a Christmas you won't forget."

"It sounds like a great experience," I said.

After Bea left, Tim and I wondered what we'd gotten ourselves into. He was usually glued to the TV watching football on Christmas, so I gave him credit for agreeing to do something different. There was no backing out now.

On Christmas Eve we went to Tim's mother's for dinner and announced our plans for the next day. They were quite amused. We promised them a full report later.

When the alarm went off at six o'clock the next morning, we questioned why we'd said yes to helping. We weren't ready to get out of bed that early on a holiday. Sleeping late and enjoying a leisurely breakfast sounded much more appealing. But we promised Bea we'd help, so we showered, dressed in jeans and flannel shirts, and drank our coffee in silence.

We arrived at the tavern and parked where Bea told us to. There were pickup trucks and plenty of cars already parked nearby. As soon as we walked in, we could smell the chili. Happy was stirring a large pot, and Bea came to greet us. Happy seemed thrilled to have our assistance for the day. He gave Tim an apron to put on and told him to cut up some more green peppers and onions. Without hesitation, Tim got busy.

Bea took me to the front of the bar and introduced me to Maggie and Fred, who were bartending. They barely looked up but smiled when Happy told them we'd be helping.

I'd never seen anyone eat chili at seven thirty in the morning before, but there wasn't an empty seat at the bar. Maybe these folks didn't realize how early it was. I didn't see a clock anywhere in the place.

"Try to help where these guys need you," Bea instructed. "Tables need to be bussed, and silverware is dumped right here when it's clean. You can sort the silverware and fill water glasses as needed. Folks will let you know what they want, trust me. You can take a break in the back room when you need it. Help yourself to a cinnamon roll back there."

My first request was someone at the end of the bar asking me for hot sauce. The guy knew I was new and told me just where to find it. He was one of the regulars, I guessed.

"Hey, everyone," shouted a woman sitting at the bar. "Jerry just gave me a new baseball cap for Christmas. How do you like it?" She put on the hat, and everyone cheered. It seemed early to be cheering for anything, but it *was* Christmas morning, I reminded myself.

I wished a couple dozen customers merry Christmas and kept busy refilling bowls of chili. I wasn't sure I could look at another bowl of it.

I walked back to the kitchen to check on Tim. He was frying ground beef for the chili and looked pretty happy about it. He wanted to know how I was doing.

"Everyone is happy, I'll say that," I chuckled.

"That's the idea," Bea said when she overheard me. "Here. Take these two bowls to the couple at the end of the counter." I nodded.

"Oh, thank you, miss," the gray-haired woman said as I placed the bowl in front of her. "You know this is the tenth Christmas I've spent here at Happy's. When Eddie and I first started coming here, there was enough room to dance to 'Honky Talk Christmas' that's playing now, but not anymore. It's shoulder to shoulder here nowadays."

"So, what brought you here in the first place?" I asked.

"This guy here!" she said, pointing to the older guy next to her, who I assumed was Eddie. "We met here at the bar. We each had a sob story to share, and well, the rest is history. We've been coming here ever since. Haven't we, Eddie?" He grinned and nodded as he took a sip of beer.

I smiled. "A love story that began at Happy's. How sweet!"

"Eddie always has a joke for us," she said. "They don't call this place Happy's for nothing." They chuckled.

At a table for four, I noticed two kiddos who looked anything but happy to be there.

"Hey, what's going on here? Did Santa not come to your house today?" I teased. They looked at me with wonder.

"Oh, they're just upset because we came here for the chili," the mother explained. "They wanted to stay home and play with their toys."

"Don't you like chili?" I asked the kids. They shook their heads. "No? Hmm. So, what's your favorite lunch?"

"Mom makes really good grilled cheese," the little boy answered with a smile.

"Do you like grilled cheese too?" I asked the little girl.

She nodded and grinned. "Yes, but they don't make grilled cheese here," she said.

"Well, let me see what I can do about that, okay?" I could see a hint of their smiles.

I went back to the kitchen and scoured the refrigerator. Thankfully, Happy had lots of cheese. I knew Tim made the best grilled cheese sandwiches ever, so I went over and asked him to make me a couple. He didn't ask why. I guess he assumed grilled cheese was a regular item on the menu. He went right to work, and then I explained my mission.

My mouth started watering as I cut the kids' sandwiches into small triangles. Their eyes lit up when I brought the sandwiches over, and their parents couldn't thank me enough.

When I returned to the bar, Fred was having a difficult conversation with a man who'd had too much to drink. Fred had called a cab to take him home, but the gentleman didn't appreciate that. I decided to intervene.

"Say, did you know it's Christmas?" I asked the man cheerfully. "You know there's nothing better than relaxing and having a good nap today. I know that's what I'll be doing when I leave here. If your belly is full of that good chili, I'd highly recommend taking Fred up on his offer."

Fred looked at me oddly but appreciated the support as he said, "How would you like this pretty young lady to walk you to the cab? That cold air outside is gonna feel mighty good, don't you think?"

"Well, if you put it that way, I guess I can't refuse," the man grumbled.

"Here, take my arm," I said, holding onto him as we slowly fumbled our way to the door without making a scene.

The cab driver got out of the cab like he was no stranger to this guy.

"Merry Christmas!" I said as the gentleman climbed into the cab. He smiled, and it touched my heart.

I went back inside, and Fred told me how grateful he was for my help. He said the guy often drank too much and was quite unruly at times.

I told him it was no problem and turned around to check on Tim in the kitchen. He was at the stove, stirring the pot. He looked right at home, laughing and having a good time with Happy. I took a few minutes to taste the chili and have half a cinnamon roll while I was back there. Mmm! No wonder people come here on Christmas.

By five o'clock, new folks were coming in for the evening meal, but some of those who had arrived at seven that morning were still parked in their seats. A few new workers had come in also, so Bea told us we could leave anytime and thanked us for all our help.

When we went to say goodbye to Happy, he was wishing the newcomers a merry Christmas. I'm sure he was ready to leave too after this long day, but Bea said he always stayed until the very end. He extended his arms for a big hug and told us to come back anytime for a free meal.

We were exhausted when we reached the apartment. We lit the Christmas tree and just collapsed on the couch. At some point we'd talk about the stories and experiences of the day, but not yet. We were too tired. I thought about what we'd have missed if we'd stayed home on our couch watching football. Seeing all the guests and helping to fill their tummies today was truly rewarding.

Tim and I agreed that serving others makes for the happiest Christmas of all. We'll be back next year!

Happy's Beer Chili

2 tbsp olive oil

1 diced onion

2 diced green peppers

1 pound ground beef

3 garlic cloves, minced

2 tbsp chili powder

2 tbsp cumin

1 tsp salt

½ tsp pepper

One 12-ounce can beer (lager, port, or stout)

Two 15-ounce cans diced tomatoes

One 6-ounce can tomato paste

One 15-ounce can pinto beans

One 15-ounce can black beans

One 15-ounce can kidney beans

Toppings such as sour cream, shredded cheddar cheese, tortilla chips, and jalapenos (optional)

1. In a large pot, heat the olive oil over medium heat.
2. Add the onion and green pepper, and sauté until soft, about 5 minutes.

3. Add the ground beef, and cook until brown, about 8 minutes.

4. Add the garlic, chili powder, cumin, salt, and pepper, and cook for 2 minutes.

5. Add the beer and allow it to deglaze the pan while you scrape up the bits on the bottom. Let cook for 5 minutes.

6. Add the remaining ingredients and stir. (Note: You can use just half a can of each of the beans if you're not a big fan of beans.)

7. Bring the mixture to a boil, reduce the heat, and simmer for at least 20 minutes. (The longer it cooks, the better.)

8. Add your favorite toppings.

All I Want for Christmas Is True Love

As a freelance writer for several publications, I was assigned to write about something romantic for the Valentine's Day issue of *Living Life* magazine. What did I know about romance as an almost forty-year-old woman who'd avoided long-term relationships by choice? Not much.

Shortly after being assigned the article, I received a notice in the mail about my twentieth high school reunion to take place the weekend after Thanksgiving. I hadn't been to any of the earlier reunions, mostly because I wasn't married and I had heard everyone came coupled up. My classmates would never understand that remaining single was a personal choice for me. I was pretty independent, and I didn't want to give that up.

Does true love exist? If it does, how do you find it? I'd never given those questions much thought, truthfully. I decided that a good way to research the topic would be to commit to attending my reunion so I could interview my old classmates about their experiences.

At the first night's mixer, I engaged in conversation with several couples. I found out quickly that the women had much more to say about their romantic relationships than the men did. Here's how it went.

Judy and Bud had married right after high school and never missed a reunion. They were holding hands when I joined them at their table. I explained my freelance assignment and asked them to help me with this notion of true love.

Their eyes lit up when I asked them if theirs had been love at first sight. They squeezed each other's hands tighter and described how all through grade school and high school, they couldn't bear to be apart.

"Our parents had a fit when we told them we wanted to get married after graduation," Judy noted. "But we told them if they wouldn't give us permission, we'd elope." Bud nodded in agreement.

"We celebrate our anniversary around the same time as our high school homecoming each year," he added.

"So, I take it that you believe in true love?" I wanted to confirm what I thought I was hearing.

"Well, ours is about as true as you can get," Bud gushed as he gave Judy a kiss on the cheek.

They seemed sweet together, and obviously they were inseparable if they'd loved each other since grade school.

I spotted Peggy Wilson sitting alone, so I decided to go over and chat with her. It didn't take long for her to admit she almost didn't come. She was still grieving the death of her husband a few months prior and knew it would be painful to see all the happy couples without having her true love by her side. That prompted me to ask about their fifteen-year marriage. She got a bit emotional when she told me they never went to bed angry with each other even if they had to stay up all night. When I asked how they met, her eyes lit up just as Judy and Bud's had.

"We met on a blind date and immediately hit it off. He called me the next day and the following days until we were never apart."

I smiled before asking, "So, how would you describe true love?"

"It's a feeling that comes from deep down inside of you," she answered. "We knew right away that we wouldn't be complete without each other."

"That's wonderful," I said. "Do you ever want to find that love again?"

"No," she answered firmly. "I was lucky the first time. I don't think I could find what he and I shared again."

Other classmates came over then, so I took the opportunity to get a drink at the bar. Standing alone was Harry Cole. He had been smart, good looking, and popular in high school. His wife was busy chatting with other people, so I thought I'd get his perspective on my topic.

After a bit of joking around, I finally asked, "Harry, I remember that you dated a lot of girls when we were growing up. How did you know Sally was the one for you?"

"If you recall, Sally wasn't the best-looking girl in high school, but she was smarter than all get-out. She was into saving the world, not dating, and never even gave me a look back then. Well, she went away to college and became absolutely gorgeous, but she still wouldn't have anything to do with me. I liked the challenge of winning her over."

"So, how did you get her to go out with you?" I asked.

"I figured that the only way she'd have anything to do with me is if I joined one of her groups, so I picked the one called Save the Trees," he confessed. "So much for joining a tree-hugger group for the right reasons! But I wanted to work with her and get to know her better, and this was the only way I knew how. Would you believe she was the one who ended up asking me out?"

I chuckled. "Well, it seems to have worked out! Would you describe what you two have as true love?"

"Well, it must be, or we'd have killed each other by now!" he joked. "We argue like crazy about everything, but neither one of us carries a grudge, and we make up rather quickly. I wouldn't want to be with anyone else."

I walked away thinking about his last comment.

After a fried chicken dinner with all the trimmings, Kevin and Anne Cummings sat down next to me to chat about what they'd heard I was doing. They seemed rather affectionate with each other, so I asked them what true love meant to them.

"I think it's different for everyone," Anne noted. "Don't you agree?"

"Yes and no," I responded. "We may have different expectations from a relationship, but the bottom line is that there has to be love. If the relationship doesn't have true love, it will crumble and fall away. Do the two of you believe in it?" They smiled as they looked at one another.

"Of course," Anne said with certainty. "We've had so many sad occasions in our lives that if we didn't have each other to console and comfort, I don't know how we'd have gotten through everything."

Kevin looked at her with loving eyes as she spoke and only added, "Yes, I can't imagine my life without her."

The DJ began playing music to encourage dancing, so I took that as my cue to cut out while I could. I grabbed my coat and walked by the bar. Katie and Allen were sitting there and pulled me toward them.

"Have an after-dinner drink with us before you go," they encouraged. I really wasn't in a hurry to get back to my empty hotel room, so I ordered an Amaretto on the rocks.

After they teased me a bit about still being single, I asked them how long they'd been married.

"One year," Allen answered.

"Oh, that can't be right. I went to your wedding ages ago."

They chuckled. "Well, after a while, Katie and I took what we like to consider a break," Allen explained. "We just couldn't figure out marriage the first time."

"Let's be honest with her, Allen," Katie interrupted. "One of us just wasn't ready to stop sowing their wild oats!"

"Oh, I see!" I said with a wink.

"It was a pretty nasty divorce," Katie noted.

"Yeah, I'll say," Allen added.

"So, what happened?"

"That saying about you can't live with them but you can't live without them fit us pretty well," Katie laughed. "We couldn't leave each other alone, even after the divorce. So, after a couple of years, Allen asked me out on a real date."

"And how did that go?" I asked.

"It was awkward for sure," Katie said, shaking her head. "But it didn't take long, and we were in each other's arms like long-lost friends. A month later he proposed, and here we are together again!"

"That's wonderful," I cheered.

"She's always been my true love, even when we were apart," Allen said as he gave Katie a hug.

We chatted a while longer as I finished my drink, and then I bid them adieu until our next reunion. As I drove away, I knew I had more material than I needed for my article. When I arrived back at my hotel room, I glanced at the few notes I'd taken. All the couples I'd talked to believed in true love and felt they'd found it with their spouses. I'd committed myself to being single long ago, but after hearing their stories, I started wondering what I might have been missing all these years.

Christmas was my favorite time of year, and it would be here in a few weeks. I knew I was blessed and happy with my friends, my family, and my work, but what if this year I, too, found true love? I suppose there would be no harm in asking Santa. Perhaps someone was out there waiting for me. How about it, Santa?

BELIEVE

We all want to believe.

Believe that the holidays will bring joy and peace.

Believe that our health will improve.

Believe that our problems will be solved.

Believe that there's a reason for what's happened.

Believe that we'll know best.

Believe that we can trust those in charge.

Believe in our US Constitution.

Believe that we'll be safe.

Believe that we're being told the truth.

Believe that we're truly loved.

Believe in our chosen faith.

Believe in our worth.

Believe that the money will be there for us.

If we believe, we'll have the best gift of all this Christmas.

The Empty Chair

We're told all the time to remember those who are no longer with us. At Christmas and Thanksgiving, Granny would always pray for those who had died. We also kept an empty chair for them.

When Grandpa passed away a few years ago, Granny could hardly hold back her tears as she recalled their very first Christmas together. It was a story we hadn't heard before. We listened intently so we could plant the details in our memories. We wanted to remember as if it was our own story to tell.

Granny passed recently, so she was on our minds this year as we gazed at the empty chair before us at our Christmas feast. After we prayed, we began sharing memories of her.

"I remember how much Granny loved Christmas," I said, tearing up.

"Oh, that's for sure!" added my brother Lou, who was visiting from New York. "She always made sure I got a card, a flannel shirt, and her famous fruitcake." Everyone chuckled at the memory of the fruitcake Granny made without fail every Christmas. "I knew I'd miss that this year, which is why I decided to come home to be with all of you."

"Well, Lou," I began, "Sarah and I decided to follow Granny's fruitcake recipe this year. For better or worse, you're still getting a fruitcake."

"Oh my goodness!" Lou said, surprised. "Granny would love that you continued her tradition!"

"I don't think Grandpa ever ate a bite of that fruitcake, if I'm remembering correctly," I joked.

"You're right, Anne. I never saw him take a bite of it," Sarah nodded, laughing. "That was just more for us. I hope our fruitcake turned out all right. It was hard to read some of her writing on the recipe card."

"I miss Granny too," my husband, Ben, chimed in. "She was never too busy cooking to take time to ask me what I was doing at work."

"Well, I knew we'd miss her Christmas Jell-O recipe, too, so we made that also," Sarah added. "It looks the same as hers, but I don't know how it'll taste."

"There's only one way to find out," Ben said. "Let's dig in!"

That we did. As we ate our Christmas Jell-O and fruitcake alongside our ham and side dishes, I occasionally looked over to the end of the table, as if Granny were still sitting in her chair. I had a feeling she was smiling from above, knowing that her special foods were still being passed around our table.

We filled that empty chair with memories of the one we missed and would forever love. Who do you see in your empty chair this Christmas?

Granny's Christmas Jell-O Salad

6 ounces lime Jell-O

5 cups hot water, divided

4 cups cold water, divided

3 ounces lemon Jell-O

½ cup mini marshmallows

8 ounces cream cheese

8 ounces crushed pineapple with juice

1 can heavy whipping cream

1 cup mayonnaise

6 ounces cherry Jell-O

1. In a bowl, add 2 cups of the hot water. Add the lime Jell-O and stir well to dissolve. Add 2 cups of the cold water and stir. Pour into a 14 × 10 × 2-inch glass pan. Chill until partially set.

2. In the top of a double boiler over high heat, add 1 cup of the hot water. Add the lemon Jell-O and stir well to dissolve. Add the marshmallows and stir to melt. Remove from the heat and cool slightly. Pour over the lime layer and chill until partially set.

3. In a bowl, place the cream cheese.

4. Drain the pineapple, reserving the juice. Add 1 cup of pineapple juice to the cream cheese. Beat until well blended, and then stir in the pineapple. Whip the cream, and then fold it, along with the mayonnaise, into the cream cheese mixture. Chill until thickened.

5. Pour the pineapple mixture onto the layer of lemon Jell-O. Chill until almost set.

6. In a bowl, add the remaining 2 cups of hot water. Add the cherry Jell-O and stir well to dissolve. Add the remaining 2 cups of cold water, and chill until syrupy. Pour the cherry Jell-O over the pineapple layer, and chill until firm.

Serves 24

Christmas Eve in Jail

~ ❦ ~

It was Christmas Eve, and I was on duty with Officer Bill Woodson. We paired up because severe weather was expected for the holiday weekend. We never knew what to expect in our small town of Evergreen located near a major interstate.

This time of year, we tried to go easy on tickets and just give warnings so we wouldn't dampen anyone's holiday spirit. But we had to bring in the most unexpected guest. Santa had been driving while intoxicated. Where was his lead reindeer when he needed him?

Working during the holidays wasn't easy, especially because it meant being away from family. Fortunately, I had a great partner. Officer Woodson, or Woody, was a confirmed bachelor who happily volunteered to take extra shifts for such occasions so that others could be with their families. Despite the big ego he developed from being tall, dark, and handsome, when it came to protecting his partner, he was professional and generous. Thanks to him, I was able to sit in the audience to watch my son Luke in his first school play earlier in the week.

Now that the sun had turned in for the night, the temps were hovering in the low twenties. Woody and I had just picked up a couple cups of hot coffee when we noticed a car pulled off to the side of an isolated road. The driver's car battery had died, and his phone had run out of juice. He told us he'd been there about twenty minutes and was getting quite cold. We gave him a jump, and he was on his way.

The next call wasn't totally unexpected. We often had phone calls from the Blakely residence because Mr. Blakely was an alcoholic and frequently became angry and abusive with his wife. But by the time we arrived, Mrs. Blakely told us all was well, and she was sorry to have bothered us. Her husband had passed out and would sleep off his temper and the alcohol for the next twelve hours or so. We never knew what to expect when we answered domestic calls like this. I was happy this one ended peacefully.

Within ten minutes of leaving the Blakelys, we watched the station wagon right in front of us slide into a ditch. Another car swerved to avoid the accident and continued on its way. We pulled behind the station wagon to see how we could help. The man exited the car with some help, but the mother, three children, and a barking dog they called Sam remained inside. It was obvious that the mom and kids were shaken up, and the dog was spooked.

Apparently they were on their way to her grandmother's house, still a good two hundred miles away. They chose to travel at night so that the young kids could pass the time by sleeping. The father had been nodding off and slid on a patch of ice.

Woody immediately took charge and called for a tow truck. Unfortunately, we learned there had been numerous slide-offs in the past couple of hours and there wouldn't be a truck available until morning. I told Woody we couldn't leave this family in the car overnight, and there wasn't much open. We had no choice but to bring them all back to the station until morning.

The mother looked grateful when we spelled out our plan. She was freezing cold and just wanted her family safe and warm. We learned the parents were Tom and Rita, and their children were Joseph (age 2), Henry (age 4), and Abraham (age 6).

Awkwardly, the entire family, including Sam, crammed into the police car. The children climbed onto Tom and Rita's laps in the back seat, and I took Sam up front with me. Henry and Abraham started chattering about getting to ride in the police car, and Joseph kept rubbing his eyes. It was past his bedtime. Fortunately, we weren't far from the police station, and Captain Everett was there to welcome us at the door. Woody had called and given him a heads-up about our visitors when we were on our way.

I assisted the family in making themselves at home in the adjacent empty cells. Joseph went right to sleep even with Henry and Abraham squealing with delight that they'd have a bedroom tonight with bars. Squealing wasn't the usual reaction we got in the station, but this was an unusual situation indeed!

Abraham noticed right away that Santa was sleeping in one of the cells. He went into panic mode, wondering how Santa would be able to deliver presents from jail. I assured the boys that Santa needed to rest tonight and tried to distract them with hot chocolate.

After about twenty minutes, it was easy to convince Rita and the boys to rest, but Tom was worried about leaving their luggage and Christmas presents in the car. Woody finally agreed to take him back to the car to retrieve whatever he wanted.

The weather continued to get worse. Temperatures had dropped further, and the snow looked to be about four inches deep. I was glad Woody and Tom didn't have to drive far to get back to the station wagon.

When the kids were asleep and Rita was brushing her teeth, I called the twenty-four-hour diner about preparing breakfast for all of us in the morning. Shirley's Café had great food, and they were always generous with us. Shirley was happy to accommodate our needs for tomorrow.

By two o'clock in the morning, all was quiet in the station except the guy in the red suit with the long white beard. He was finally sobering up. We told him we'd release him by noon if he agreed to play Santa in the morning for the kiddos. The gifts were under our Christmas tree by the captain's desk, so all he had to do was pass them out. He seemed relieved he wouldn't have to spend another night in jail.

Woody and I prayed we wouldn't be called out any more for the night. Fortunately, with the snowstorm, most folks were staying home.

Woody took Sam out a couple times so he wouldn't disturb the others. I knew that the minute I dozed off, the little ones would begin to stir. We sure didn't expect a Christmas Eve like this!

Joseph, the two-year-old, was the first to awaken, and Henry and Abraham followed shortly thereafter. They remembered quickly that it was Christmas morning and wondered what Santa had brought them. When Santa saw the kids up and about, he arose with a hearty "Ho! Ho! Ho!" that made the children scream with delight. Their screams grew even louder when Santa gave them their gifts. This was a day they wouldn't soon forget.

In the middle of the commotion, Officer Miller brought in two men who were cold, tired, hungry, and without homes. I poured them some coffee while Woody left to retrieve the food from the diner.

When Woody arrived with the food, it was a party to behold. Shirley had outdone herself with strata; strips of bacon; fried potatoes; baked apples; and coffee, milk, and juice. No one would be going hungry today!

As we were finishing breakfast and the kids were playing with the toys they'd just received, the tow-truck company called to say they were ready to send a truck. Woody informed the family that it was time for them to be on their way and continue their trip to Grandma's. We exchanged hugs, gave a few last pets to Sam, and wished them all safe travels. Santa told the kids to be kind to each other, and he'd see them again next year.

I was almost sad to see everyone leave. This was a Christmas that none of us would forget. I hope we created some good memories for this wonderful family. I guess Santa was meant to be here for the kids' sake. He promised us he'd be back again next year, but sober and without need for a bed.

Shirley's Strata

6 eggs

1 pound fried breakfast sausage, drained

1 tsp dry mustard

1 tsp salt

2 cups milk

½ pound shredded sharp cheese

6 slices white bread

1. Grease a 9 × 11-inch glass pan.

2. In a bowl, combine the eggs, sausage, dry mustard, salt, and milk. Add the cheese.

3. Place the bread in the pan, and pour the egg mixture on top. Refrigerate overnight.

4. Remove the dish from the refrigerator as you preheat the oven to 350° F.

5. Bake for 45 minutes.

Serves 6.

The Lady in Red

Who's the lady in red, and how did she become obsessed with that color?

Louise was enchanted with her three older sisters' fashion trends. All three wore bright red lipstick and nail polish. She wanted to be just like them.

When Louise was sick or had a friend stay over, her mother would bring out a red Irish chain quilt. She'd hug it like a long-lost friend. It didn't matter to her how tattered it was.

She also cherished a pair of bright red slippers Uncle Bill had given her for Christmas one year. She wore them for years until her heels lapped over the back.

When she and the family would visit Aunt Mary in the city, she'd admire her aunt's 1950s red plastic and chrome kitchen set in the breakfast room. The windows behind the table had sills lined with an assortment of red-and-white salt and pepper shakers. Louise would sit at the table trying to decide which pair was her favorite.

Before Louise started school, her passion for red got her in trouble a few times. One day she took her sister Marilyn's red nail polish and painted all the keys on the family typewriter. Another time her cousin came over to play, and the two of them locked themselves in the bathroom and painted themselves with Mercurochrome from head to toe. Needless to say, they wore the color for some time.

Starting school only enhanced Louise's love of red. She always chose to wear red clothing and shoes if she could get away with it. Her favorite teacher, Mrs. Wersig, refreshed her lipstick after recess every day. Louise watched intently and wished the color were being applied to her own lips.

Valentine's Day was one of her favorite holidays since it meant red hearts were plastered everywhere. When Charles, her crush since first grade, gave her a valentine heart saying, "Be Mine," she cherished it for a good long time.

Louise sensed her mother loved red as much as she did. Her mother's apron drawer was filled with red-and-white aprons of all kinds. Her handkerchief box had mostly red-and-white handkerchiefs that smelled like the perfume Evening in Paris, which she wore for special occasions. Dad would bring her a big red poinsettia at Christmas, which she'd put in the picture window. When her mother took Louise shopping to pick out a fancy dress for the church's Christmas program each year, she agreed with her daughter that the red, sparkly, crinkly ones were the best.

When Louise was ten, her mother decided she was old enough to learn embroidery. She gave Louise kitchen towels with designs stamped on them. Louise decided red thread was perfect for all the fruits and vegetables she stitched.

As Louise approached her teenage years, she incorporated red into her bedroom. Her favorite accessory was a small table lamp shaped like a mushroom. It was red with white polka dots on it. She kept it on her nightstand and used it as she read her favorite stories before bed.

When Louise was about to turn sixteen, her family suffered the worst imaginable tragedy. Her mother was attending a weekday church service with her dad when she suffered a severe heart attack and died immediately. Her mother had wanted her to come to church with them that day, but Louise didn't want to go. She wasn't with her mom for her last breaths, and she felt terrible guilt for it. She also felt deserted.

To cope with her mother's death, Louise began using that tattered red quilt that her mom had kept in the hall closet. It brought her comfort now, as it always had when she was sick. Tucking it firmly under her body each night felt like a tight hug from her mom. It was just what she needed to get through the sad, lonely nights.

The teachers at Louise's school recognized her grief and tried to stop rumors circulating about her dad dating a woman the age of her oldest sister. Louise was in denial, but soon she learned that the rumors were true. She felt her dad was betraying her and betraying her mom. Their house no longer felt like home, and she wanted to get away.

Louise started looking for love in all the wrong places, and many people took advantage of her. She yearned to have a home of her own, so when she met Joe, whom she respected for his education and solid financial future, she agreed to marry him at the age of twenty. She wanted to establish a home like many of her friends were doing. And she knew just the color scheme she wanted.

Shortly after her marriage to Joe, she saw a red-and-white quilt she loved at a store downtown. It was quite unusual in that it had tatted circles in each corner of redwork embroidery blocks that depicted the months of the year. It was more than she could afford, so she put it on layaway and paid on it every week until she could finally take it home two months later. She loved the feel of hand stitching as she caressed the quilt. It once again made her think of her mother. She began collecting antique red-and-white quilts after that. It didn't take long for antique dealers to call her when they'd come across one. Antiquing became a favorite pastime for her and her husband.

As quilting became the rage, so did Louise's interest in the industry. In her late twenties, she decided to open a quilting and needlework business.

Because she had always enjoyed working with her hands, the surge of redwork interested her. As busy as she was, she managed to make many quilts using the redwork technique. She began researching the history of what was known as Turkey red. Turkey red became dye fast in the 1880s, appealing to quiltmakers who were worried about the red fading. It was called Turkey red because it was developed in Turkey. Its delicious hue was found in the many antique quilts Louise was collecting and selling. Louise even started a redwork group among some women who shared her love of the color.

As Louise started collecting various red-and-white textiles, she couldn't ignore what was happening in the button industry. When she visited a button shop in New York, she knew she had to incorporate them into her business also. She personally collected plastic red-and-white buttons, as well as red glass.

Christmas was always Louise's favorite time of year. Customers and friends knew her love for red and white and began gifting her ornaments in those colors. It didn't take long for her to have enough to fill a tree. No two were alike, and she knew the history of each one.

The most unusual collection Louise acquired was embroidered splashers. No one seemed to know what they were. When she learned they were made at the turn of the century to protect the wallpaper in front of the wash bowls and basins, she became fascinated. The splashers were quite elaborate considering their utilitarian purpose. Louise loved educating others about them.

Word was getting out about this lady in red. People asked her to lecture, write articles, and even write books about her knowledge. It was obvious she was living her dream.

Let it be said: The lady in red is me!

Christmas Nuts and Bolts

(A must-have favorite with my family at Christmastime)

6 tbsp butter

4 tsp Worcestershire sauce

⅜ tsp garlic powder

6 cups Chex cereal (a mix of different flavors as desired)

1 jar dry-roasted peanuts

½ cup any size pretzels

1. Preheat oven to 250° F.

2. Pour melted butter into shallow baking pan. Stir in Worcestershire sauce and garlic powder.

3. Add Chex, peanuts, and pretzels. Mix till well coated.

4. Roast in oven for a total of 45 minutes, Stir every 15 minutes.

5. Spread onto paper towels to cool.

Yields about 8 cups.

White Gull Inn's Oatmeal Christmas Cookies

1½ cups (3 sticks) butter, softened

1½ cups of Door County maple syrup

1 cup sugar

2 large eggs

2½ tsp of vanilla extract

6 cups old-fashioned rolled oats

2 cups flour

2 tsp baking soda

½ tsp salt

1. Preheat oven to 350° F.

2. Spray 2 baking sheets with nonstick cooking oil.

3. In a large bowl, with an electric mixer, beat together butter, maple syrup, sugar, eggs, and vanilla.

4. Stir in oats.

5. In a separate bowl, stir together flour, baking soda, and salt.

6. Add dry ingredients to cream mixture and mix well.

7. Drop by rounded teaspoons about 2 inches apart on prepared baking sheets.

8. Bake 12–15 minutes.

Yields about 6 dozen.

GOODBYE TO CHRISTMAS!

The lights disappear after Christmas sails by.

The season's carols, wishes, and gifts fade with a sigh.

What's next is wrapping up a good or bad year.

One welcomes the next and toasts it with cheer.

Resolutions and wishes are expressed with great hope.

One prays for good health and patience to cope.

Our dreams and great plans we've made for the year

Are sometimes short-lived as the months draw near.

Never give up as you start the new year,

It's just three-hundred-some days till Christmas is here!

Happy New Year!

If you like these short stories, you'll love Ann Hazelwood's novels. Read on for a preview of *Quilters of the Door*, the first of the Door County Quilts series.

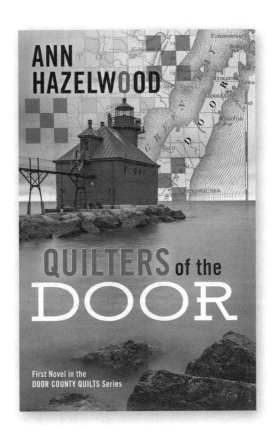

Chapter 1

"Claire Elizabeth Stewart," I said aloud as I drove along Interstate 55, "what are you doing?" I had so many thoughts going through my mind. Then I spotted a rest stop ahead. That just might provide me with a good place to turn around. I took a deep breath, activated my turn signal, and veered into the rest stop parking lot. I parked carefully since I was not accustomed to pulling a U-Haul. I got out of the car and looked at the container on wheels that carried the greater part of my most prized possessions. The air was chilly, so I rushed inside to get warm and to call Cher for some assurance. Thankfully, she answered quickly.

"Claire, what's up? Where are you now?" Cher asked.

"I'm at a rest stop off of Highway 55," I responded, feeling even more uneasy. "I think this just might be a crazy idea."

"Not again, for heaven's sake," Cher said, feigning an exasperated moan. "We've gone over everything a hundred times! It's normal for you to feel anxious. There are a lot of unknowns when moving to a new community, but it can be exciting, too!"

"Really?"

"Look, you already have a place to stay, and there's a new friend just waiting to meet you. I left some basic things for you until you can decide what to do permanently."

"I know, I know."

"You're arriving in Door County during the perfect season. I heard that the colors are at their peak. Fall was always my favorite time of year there." She paused. "What are you so worried about?"

"Well, leaving my mother, for starters, and to be honest, I'm not kidding myself about the fact that I'm running away from Austen, too."

"Your mother is fine. I'll check in on her. You know I will. Remember, she was all for you moving to Wisconsin. Forget Austen. He's obviously moved on, and so should you. The mere fact that he never came for you after you left is pretty telling, isn't it?"

"It is," I responded, feeling a familiar ache return. "I still can't believe I had the nerve to move out when he was at that medical conference, but if he had been anywhere around, I couldn't have done it."

"Look, Claire Bear, you'd better be on your way. Ericka will be looking for you. I gave you her cell number, so keep her informed if your plans change. You'll have everything you need when you get there."

"Yes, Cher Bear, I have everything," I lamented. "I have everything but confidence." I took a deep breath to calm myself. "How is your mom today?"

"She's pretty much out of it. Every day is different, but thanks for asking."

"You're a good daughter to have moved back to Perryville

to take care of her."

"And you're a good friend to take my place in Door County off my hands. It's perfect for an artist. You'll love it there, I promise."

"Okay, Cher Bear, if you say so. Remember, I can't promise that I'll buy your place until I've stayed there for a few months."

"I know. I'm not worried. You'd better be on your way now. I love you!"

"I love you, too!"

Cher and I had grown up together and attended the same schools. In elementary school, our fellow classmates called us Claire Bear and Cher Bear. As we grew older, we were the only ones who continued the tradition. It was a shared connection to our past. Cher and I had also attended art school together. When Cher married, she'd moved to Green Bay, Wisconsin. I missed her very much, but we texted or talked almost daily. Her marriage had fizzled after a couple of years, so she'd moved to Door County, a haven for artists up and down the peninsula. She'd pursued her art career much more than I had through the years. The thought of setting up my little studio where Cher had lived did seem exciting. From pictures she'd sent, the little village of Fish Creek appeared to be very charming.

I got a Diet Dr. Pepper out of a soda machine before I climbed back in my white Subaru. Cher had said that I had the perfect automobile for Wisconsin, so that was reassuring. As I got closer and closer to Wisconsin, I could see that it was going to be a beautiful state with charming barns and numerous signs urging me to buy cheese. I was blessed with light traffic on the journey, so it was easy for my eyes to wander across the landscape. All the while, I had many uncertainties running through my head. Would Austen ever know I had moved away? If so, would he care where? Austen was Dr. Austen Page, a pediatrician in Perryville, Missouri. True and simple, he was idolized by many. When I'd met him, I hadn't known that he was a doctor. He enjoyed being with someone who had local connections. After knowing him for just a few months, I'd moved in with him. His home was lovely and provided me with a beautiful studio where I could make my painted wall quilts. I felt sure that I would never have that kind of opportunity again. In the beginning, it had been idyllic.

However, as time went on, it was evident that Austen did not want to get married. For the most part, I'd felt the same way, particularly at first. He seemed to really enjoy attending frequent social engagements with me and bragged about my abilities as an artist when we were out with others. I was fortunate in that many of his friends purchased my work.

My mother, Mary Elizabeth Stewart, was not happy about our relationship and never let me forget it. She would comment about how folks would talk, saying they would ask her point-blank if Austen and I were going to get married. I knew she wanted security for me. She often warned that my life would be incredibly challenging if I found I had to support myself in my mid-fifties. Mom was always nice to Austen, but he was perceptive enough to know how she felt about the marriage issue.

As the years progressed, I'd realized that I was spending more and more time alone. Austen and I socialized less and less. Our conversations became less and less frequent. I began to feel restless and unfulfilled in the relationship.

It was just undeniably clear that I needed to move on. Austen happened to be away at a four-day medical conference in Chicago. I knew it was the perfect time to move out without his interference.

Mom was pleased when I chose to move in with her. I waited and waited for Austen to call or come to talk with me, but he never did. I was hurt, but I knew it was the perfect way for us to end the relationship. After all that time together, there was nothing more to say, really. To her credit, Mom was kind enough not to say "I told you so."

In the midst of my deciding what to do next, Cher had announced that she was coming back to Perryville to take care of her mother, who was in the beginning stages of Alzheimer's disease. She also had a few other health issues, but Cher was adamant that she could provide the care her mother needed.

Even though I was the one to initiate the breakup with Austen, I still felt the sting of a failed relationship. Cher was the first to suggest that I move to Door County and take over her place. At first, I thought the idea was crazy, but I also thought it sounded perfect for my personal life as well as my little quilt business. I agreed to make the move even before telling Mom. I'd never forget the disappointed look on her face. After we talked, I assured her that Cher would be around if she needed help. Despite her own personal sadness at my decision, she was able to give me a hug and a smile of approval. Even now as I drove into unfamiliar territory, I remembered the warmth of her smile just as I entered Door County, Wisconsin.

Chapter 2

As soon as I crossed the bridge into an area that I would later learn was called Southern Door, the foliage became strikingly colorful. Sturgeon Bay, the largest town in Door County, was about to greet me. My destination of Fish Creek would take me on Route 42, which eventually snaked to the west side of the peninsula. I looked forward to exploring the east side in the future. To my left were the waters of Green Bay and to my right was Lake Michigan. The area was richly dotted with marinas. I slowed my speed, not wanting to miss a thing!

I loved seeing the many signs welcoming me to the charming "Door," as locals called it. When I saw a billboard for the Door County Coffee and Tea Company, I knew I had to stop. I was ready for a break, and I knew from Cher how popular their coffee was. Near Carlsville, I saw the beautiful white building on the left side of the road. I knew from the attractive fall blossoms and pumpkins that they used for decorations that I was in for a real treat.

As I entered, I recalled that the enterprise was a family-owned company and had been a Door County tradition since 1993. There was a café where I could order a cup of coffee and choose from a number of baked items showcased under a glass counter. There was no question that I had entered a world of cherries! There was cherry crumb coffee cake, cherry muffins, cherry nut cookies, cherry scones, and, of course, cherry pie. I asked the server to give me one of each! After all, what do we do when in Rome? When it came to coffee, I ordered cherry creme. Where else would I get such a unique coffee flavor?

While I waited for my order, I glanced towards a glass display wall that allowed me to see firsthand how the coffee was produced. I could have stood there all day! I watched the organized process with an odd sense of pride, somehow sensing that this new-to-me Door County would be my home.

After I paid for and collected my goodies, I ventured to the other side of the spacious store. Walls of packaged coffee and tea were displayed, enticing me to consider an additional purchase. As I took my first sip of the cherry creme coffee, I quickly picked up a package of it to enjoy in the cabin. I'd found my favorite coffee on my first trip to the store!

As I shopped around a bit, I saw that the store carried a variety of Door County souvenirs and a lovely array of shirts and clothing. I had always been a sucker for these types of items, but I tried to exercise some degree of restraint. After all, I hadn't even arrived at my destination yet, but the items certainly held my attention. There were cherries on so many of the selections. These items would be great to remember when it came time for Christmas shopping! Repeatedly, I had to remind myself that I was traveling and that I could not spend hours looking at everything.

As I stood in line to pay for my purchases, I noticed how it seemed as if every single person was so happy. The sales staff was pleasant, and the customers were excited to be there. I figured that this was the perfect place to stop as you entered the "Door," as well as the perfect place to stop before leaving the area. The only good thing about departing was that when I got in my car, the aromas of my purchases permeated the air. I inhaled deeply, keenly aware that my mood was improving greatly.

Driving on, I saw numerous signs for golf courses and wineries. The Door Peninsula Winery was straight ahead. I felt sure that many vacationers traveled home with a bottle of wine from there.

The next town I came to was Egg Harbor. What a precious name for a village! Traffic was a bit heavy as I made my way, but I was grateful for a closer look at what this little village had to offer. There were darling shops and restaurants, but when I saw Main Street Market, I remembered how Cher had told me that I would likely be doing my shopping there because they had such unique foods and produce. Perhaps a quick stop might be smart, since I knew there would not be a crumb of anything in Cher's cabin.

When I walked in the door, there was a coffee bar with treats to greet me as I got my cart. The neat and tidy place was very appealing. The beautiful array of produce caused my mouth to water. Of course, I had to have a bag of cherries, and the Honeycrisp apples were right in season. I also got my staple of bananas as I headed towards the expansive aisles of wine. Cherry wine? Why not? I wasn't a sweet wine person, but who wouldn't love cherry wine? My appetite was filling my grocery cart!

I could have stayed another half hour, but I reminded myself that I still wasn't home. The attendant at the checkout lane engaged me in pleasant conversation, and the elderly man bagging my groceries insisted on carrying them out for me. I decided that I could certainly get used to this friendly, easy lifestyle.

Chapter 3

As I drove to Fish Creek, I nibbled on the cherries, which were delightful. Passing a community called Juddville, I wondered how it had gotten such a name. I saw many tucked-away galleries amid the beautiful scenery. How quaint and inspirational to have a studio in this kind of creative environment. The road to my destination was up, down, and curvy as I drove down the final hill to enter Fish Creek. My excitement and curiosity grew knowing I was minutes away from a completely fresh start.

There was a four-way stop in the center of Fish Creek. Cher had said that there were no traffic lights in Door County. As I waited my turn, I noticed that the area was teeming with pedestrian tourists. I had to take care not to run into distracted people. I glanced at Cher's instructions, which told me to turn left, but my curiosity wanted me to turn right. Obediently, I turned left and drove slowly so I could observe the shops that lined both sides of the street. The bay was to my right. I could see it as I passed a couple of streets. Cher's place must have been closer to the water than

I'd realized. My GPS indicated that I should make another left on the corner where the Church of the Atonement was situated. The charming building was no bigger than most folks' living rooms and was nestled in a wood-like setting. I knew I'd have to check it out at some later date. I saw the Cottage Row street sign at the same time as my GPS announced that I had arrived at my destination. I looked straight ahead, and there was the small log cabin that Cher had described.

I pulled into the length of the grassy drive and saw an expansive front yard edged by tall cedar trees. I stayed in the car for a moment to take it in. Would and could this be my permanent home? I got out of the car and followed the steppingstones to the entrance of the cabin. The entire front porch was enclosed by glass and screens. Cher had filled it with wicker furniture that fit the space perfectly. I then noticed a car pulling in behind my U-Haul.

"Claire?" a voice called out. A woman stepped out of the vehicle and approached me.

"Yes?" I responded.

"I'm Ericka Hansen, Cher's friend."

"Oh, yes, of course. She told me you'd meet up with me when I arrived. It's nice to meet you."

Ericka gave me a welcoming hug. Her flurry of long reddish hair and pretty smile put me at ease. "You've just arrived?" she asked. "So, what do you think? It's pretty cute, isn't it?"

"Yes, it is," I said, looking it over. "It's small, but the setting is absolutely beautiful, and it's right in the heart of Fish Creek."

"Yes, and it's great for me as well because I always have

a place to park, which is a challenge around here during the tourist season. Hey, let's get you inside. I have my key if you don't have yours handy. George, my brother, will be over later to help you unload. He knows where to take the U-Haul when it's empty."

"That is so nice of him," I said. "Who lives in the gorgeous house next door?"

Ericka smiled. "Their last name is Bittner. Their landscaping is beautiful, isn't it? They're permanent residents but they are in Florida a lot. I think you'll like them. On second thought, before we go inside, perhaps I need to walk you around the house before it gets dark," she offered.

"Sure, let's do that."

Cozy up with more quilting mysteries from Ann Hazelwood...

WINE COUNTRY QUILT SERIES

After quitting her boring editing job, aspiring writer Lily Rosenthal isn't sure what to do next. Her two biggest joys in life are collecting antique quilts and frequenting the area's beautiful wine country. The murder of a friend results in Lily acquiring the inventory of a local antique store. Murder, quilts, and vineyards serve as the inspiration as Lily embarks on a journey filled with laughs, loss, and red-and-white quilts.

THE DOOR COUNTY QUILT SERIES

Meet Claire Stewart, a new resident of Door County, Wisconsin. Claire is a watercolor quilt artist and joins a prestigious small quilting club when her best friend moves away. As she grows more comfortable after escaping a bad relationship, new ideas and surprises abound as friendships, quilting, and her love life all change for the better.